J78719

D1540085

The Haunted Classroom

BY
ZENO ZEPLIN

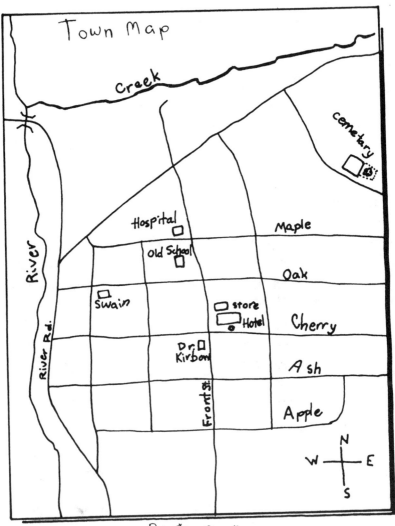

Town Map

Creek

cemetery

River

River Rd.

Hospital

Old School

Maple

Oak

Swain

store

Hotel

Cherry

Dr.
Kirban

Ash

Front St.

Apple

N
W — E
S

By Jennifer Jones

Dear Reader:

Warning!!! This is a Book of Haunting Happenings and **more**.

The fourth grade classroom is truly haunted — — or is it? — — by whom?

A report for social studies by two students in the class reveals an enchanting mystery of unusual local history. It suggests the presence of a ghost in that old classroom — — and WOW! Eerie things begin to happen there; excitement turns to fear. A secret class *plan* is made. A trap is set. The trap is tripped. **Eiee!!!** — — **What is this?** — — **What is that?** Fuzzy as a tombstone is the key.

A jig, a laugh, the class whistles in, then one screams out, pursued by cascading ancient crystal orbs. There is panic, — — the sheriff, — — a meeting of worried parents called, — — and woe galore.

A quiet **Observation** triggers a sudden exciting **Revelation** that leads to **Jubilation**; it all happens in between, and it's **wilder, stranger, spookier** than any two halloweens in **THE HAUNTED CLASSROOM.**

Read it — — right away — — if you dare!

Now remember this very, very well. *The secret is sacred,* so dread to spoil and fear to tell. Only these words I've just said should ever be told — — and only to the bold. These very words alone — and nothing — **nothing more.** Beware *The Killjoy Curse!!!*

Beware, Beware,

Zeno Zeplin

OTHER BOOKS
by ZENO ZEPLIN
Illustrated by JUDY JONES

THE CROSS-EYED GHOST

Keith and two friends investigate a mysterious ghostly light. Its eerie floating path around a solitary old chimney means trouble for those who encounter it.

To read - agaes 10-14. Read aloud - 8 and up

SECRETS OF SILVER VALLEY

A southwestern mystery and adventure story about an unusual Hispanic family.

To read - ages 7-12. Read aloud - age 6 and up

POPCORN IS MISSING

A Katy and Beth mystery. The Town Clowns are Popcorn & Jody. After a delightful performance at the supermarket, Popcorn, a little dog, is missing. Katy and Beth search for clues and rescue Popcorn.

To read - ages 7-10. Read aloud - age 4 and up

SECRET MAGIC

Lauren must start fifth grade far from home with no friends and no hair. Magic is created with secrets, giving her the love and friendship to cope.

To read - ages 9-14. Read aloud - age 7 and up

GREAT TEXAS CHRISTMAS LEGENDS

Five enchanting stories of Christmas Texana for the whole family. Legends of historical places, trains, ships, cowboys, Indians, shrimp boats and more.

For ages 9 to 90. Read aloud - age 7 and up

The Haunted Classroom

BY
ZENO ZEPLIN

Illustrated by
Judy Jones

NEL-MAR
Publishing

First Edition 1989

Copyright 1989
Nelson E. Eberspacher

Zeplin, Zeno, 1925 -
    The Haunted Classroom / by Zeno Zeplin ; illustrated by Judy Jones. — 1st ed.
        p. cm.
    Summary: Following the fourth grade class's history reports, eerie happenings occur in their classroom, suggesting the presence of a ghost.
    ISBN 0-9615760-8-1 : $11.95.
    ISBN 0-9615760-9-X (pbk.) : $6.95
    [1. Ghosts—Fiction. 2. Schools—Fiction. 3. Mystery and detective stories.] I. Jones, Judy (Judy E.), ill. II. Title.
PZ7.Z43Hau   1989
Fic—dc20
                                                                89-9422
                                                                   CIP
                                                                    AC

                                                    ISBN # 0-9615760-9-X
NEL-MAR Publishing
HC-2, Box 267-C   ISBN # 0-9615760-8-1
Canyon Lake, Texas 78133   Printed in the U.S.A.

ACKNOWLEDGEMENT

The imagination that created this story began when students in Floresville Elementary School, Floresville, Texas, asked for a story "just for the fourth grade." To those students and their teacher, Mrs. Ann Rhew, our special thanks for the inspiration and for helping with editing the story and suggesting names for the book.

We are also indebted to the following students and teachers for their specific involvement with encouragement, excitement, editing and suggesting names for the book:

Fourth Grades at Mountain Valley Elementary, Sattler, Texas
    Teacher - Margaret Speck
Beyond the Classroom Students at St. Andrews Episcopal School, Austin, Texas
    Director - Pam Craig
Academically Able Third Grade Reading Class at E. A. Poe Elementary, Houston, Texas
    Teacher - Glenda Kelly

To all the many schools we have visited to discuss the importance, the methods and the adventures of writing, we gratefully acknowledge the shared insights, imagination and contagious enthusiasm of faculty and students. Theirs is a magic land where the good life really has its beginnings.

We are especially grateful to Shanna Lee Smith, fourth grade student, Floresville, Texas, for suggesting THE HAUNTED CLASSROOM for this book's title.

Last, but not least, thanks to Beth Fallon, Jennifer Jones, Jason Zeplin and Jennifer Lopez, our first young editors, and Teri Gordon, Margy Eberspacher and Claryce Holcombe our senior editors.

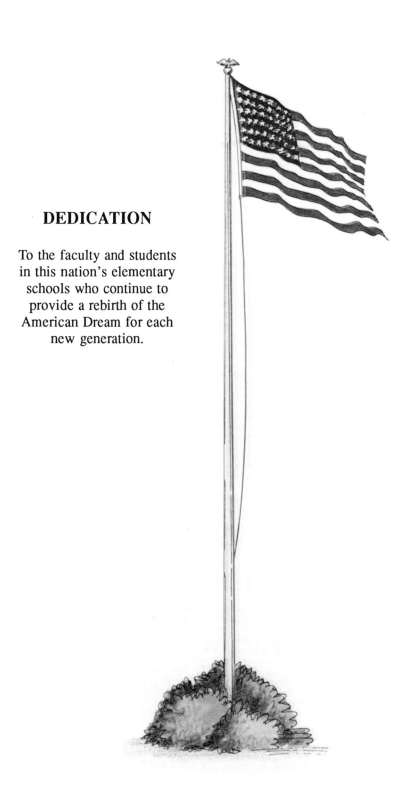

DEDICATION

To the faculty and students in this nation's elementary schools who continue to provide a rebirth of the American Dream for each new generation.

TABLE OF CONTENTS

CHAPTER 1

The Doggone Assignment

FRIDAY

David could hardly wait. His dad had promised him one of Mr. Dean's new collie puppies if he did well on his math test. The paper with the big red "94" on it neatly folded into his shirt pocket was a sure ticket for his pick of the pups. Those little dogs are at their loving and playful best. School will be out any minute now, he thought.

"I need your attention, class. Attention . . . attention! Look at me, David, so I'll know you are listening," said Miss Wilson. "Monday, we begin our studies of local history and we'll start with the reports from David and Karen. On Tuesday, Annie and Stephen will report. Be ready."

1

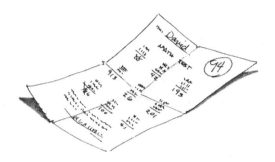

David's dream was shattered. He wasn't ready for Monday. Why does homework take the fun out of everything, he thought. There is just no way to make a history report out of plans for a new puppy.

The bell rang. As David began to gather his coat and books, Chester White came across the room to David's desk.

With a sneer, Chester looked down at David. "Don't give us another silly sissy report about a woolly worm or whatever it was," he said with a sarcastic laugh.

"A gypsy moth," corrected David, staring him in the eye. "Now crawl on out of here, Chester."

Chester headed out the door and down the stairs still muttering insults at David's last report.

"Do you have anything ready?" asked Karen, as she caught up with David.

"No."

"Neither do I," said Karen. She took a deep breath and let it out in a long disgusted sigh.

David and Karen were the last out of the room, both silent in thought. David stared at the deeply worn treads on the wooden stairs as they made their way quietly out of the building. Their common problem kept them together.

2

David looked up and down the street. Since there was no sign of his mother or their station wagon, he started across the street toward the bench where he waited for her in good weather. Karen walked with him as she headed toward her house. They stared dismally at the ground. David kicked at a rock and Karen giggled when he missed it.

There on the bench sat an old man with a walking cane in his hand. His thin white hair was gleaming in the sun. David and Karen stopped beside him.

"Children," he said. "Would you help me find the lens out of my glasses? When I sneezed, they fell onto this bench and one lens came out. I can't find it."

"Sure," said both kids together.

They put their books on the end of the bench and began to search.

"Here it is," said Karen. "It bounced way over here onto the grass."

"Oh, thank you," the old man said gratefully.

"Here, let me see if it will go back into the frame," said David. "Nope, the little screw is missing, Sir, but you can get that fixed, the lens is okay."

"My name is Ben Swain," the old man said as he held out his hand.

"I am David Diven," said David, shaking Mr. Swain's hand, "and this is my friend, Karen Murphy."

"Pleased to meet you both, and thanks for helping me with the glasses. Diven . . . Diven, yes, I knew a boy named Tom Diven years ago."

"My father is Tom Diven," said David, smiling.

"Let's see," said Mr. Ben thoughtfully as he sat down on the bench again, "Tom married a pretty red-headed girl named Nancy, yes, Nancy Decker. That right?"

"She's my mother. I'm waiting for her now."

"She loved dolls, I ordered special dolls for Nancy," said Mr. Ben fondly. "But, Murphy, I'm not remembering any Murphys."

"My father didn't grow up here, but my mother was Corey Mitchell," said Karen.

"Oh my, yes," he said smiling and nodding, "I knew little Corey with the long blond hair, green eyes and dimples in her cheeks when she smiled, and I think I remember a freckle or two. Now, her brother Mike liked to whistle. You could hear Mike whistling a block away. They were great kids."

"Where did you know them, Mr. Swain?" asked David.

"I owned the old general store that used to be right over where the hospital is now," he said.

"We haven't seen you before," said Karen. "Do you still live here?"

"Yes, three blocks down, but I usually walk the other way. Today I wanted to come over here to remember my first store and the old hotel that once stood there where your school is now."

David and Karen looked at one another and each knew what the other was thinking.

"Mr. Swain," said David, "we have to tell about some local history in class Monday. Would you tell us more about things that were here long ago, please?"

"Oh, please," begged Karen.

"Kids, everybody calls me Mr. Ben. Won't you do that too? Now, asking me to remember is like asking the sun to shine on a pretty day. Of course, I'll tell you some of the interesting things I was thinking about just before I dropped my glasses. How much time do you have?"

"Well, until my mother comes," said David excitedly, "and she will wait some. She's like that, and she'll take Karen home too, so that she won't be too late.

CHAPTER 2

A History Mystery

FRIDAY After School

Mr. Ben smiled as he studied David and Karen a thoughtful moment. Their eagerness seemed to inspire him.

"All right then," said Mr. Ben, as he leaned back to get comfortable. "Do you want to hear about my first store, the tornado, the old hotel, or the Indian chief and his ghost?"

Karen clapped her hands in excitement. "All of it," she said.

"The Indian chief and his ghost!" exclaimed David, "I gotta know about that."

"Well," said Mr. Ben, as he pointed across the street with his walking cane, "about where the flagpole is, no, just a bit beyond it, is where my first store was. It was a wooden building with a tin roof and a facade on this street."

"What's a facade?" asked Karen.

"Oh, that is just the face or front of a building that can be seen from the street. Often a store has a big fancy front to dress it up and give the merchant a big place to put his sign." Mr. Ben held his cane above his head in both hands to demonstrate the sign.

"Like the theater?" asked Karen.

"Yes, or like the furniture store over there." He pointed again with his cane. "See the big sign up over the doors and the fancy gallery posts and beautiful windows outside, but inside it is just a plain large open building with furniture everywhere. The facade or front of my old store faced here on Front Street like all the stores in the town did back then," said Mr. Ben.

"Well, now we know how Front Street got its name," said Karen.

"Most old towns had a Front Street. Some towns later changed the names to Main Street or even First Street," explained Mr. Ben. "I rented that building for my store and my sign read, 'Ben's Town Market.' The Travelers' Hotel was next door, right where the schoolhouse is now. The old gray building had porches upstairs and downstairs all the way across the front. The windows were tall, the curtains inside were made of white lace. Smoke from the wood stoves in the rooms and the kitchen would swirl up on a cold day or a still night."

"Did you have electric lights back then?" asked David.

"Oh no," said Mr. Ben, "but there were always

kerosene lanterns hanging on each side of the front door of the old hotel. Inside everyone used candles or kerosene lamps. You know, as I think about it now, it looked a little spooky even then."

"Spooky?" exclaimed Karen. "Is that where the ghost was?"

"Yes, eventually, but we're not to that yet."

"Tell us about the ghost," pleaded David, as he squirmed with anticipation.

"In due time, David," said Mr. Ben. "First, you need to know how the ghost came about."

Karen took her books off the bench, placed them on the sidewalk and sat on them. From there she could look up at Mr. Ben's face and see his eyes and the expressions of his delightful old face as he began to tell his story.

"One spring about 1915, an old man checked into the hotel and signed the register with a simple 'X'. Now that wasn't too unusual because many folks who couldn't read and write did that back then," said Mr. Ben. "In fact more than half, maybe three fourths could write their name and read only a little. Only a few people could read as well as you do now."

"But we're only in the fourth grade," explained Karen in amazement.

"Well, I guessed that from the sound and looks of you, even without my glasses. I have a great-grandson about your age and he reads to me better than most grownups could read back then."

"Miss Wilson, our teacher, told us we read about as well as the average person now," said Karen.

"Just think how smart you can be by the time you graduate from school," said Mr. Ben.

"Yes, Sir," said David. "But, tell me about the

ghost. I need that for social studies class Monday."

Mr. Ben chuckled and smiled as he rubbed his chin in thought. "Now this old man dressed about like most folks, but he was obviously an Indian. He had very long black hair, brown eyes and a kindly, but craggy old face with a big nose. Beyond a nod and a simple 'yes' or 'no', he said very little. But when he looked at you, you felt he knew all about you."

"What was his name?" asked Karen.

"When asked, he mumbled something no one could understand; so we just called him 'Chief' or 'Chief Longhair,'" explained Mr. Ben. "He had Room 8 upstairs in the hotel. He would eat stew or barbecue at the hotel dining room. The rest of the time he ate

jerky and crackling bread which he bought at my store. And sometimes he would cook a rabbit over an open fire under an old tree behind the hotel. Since he had no gun, and no bow and arrow, we never knew how he caught the rabbits."

"What is crackling bread?" asked David.

"Remember I told you we had no electricity back then. There were no refrigerators nor freezers, so we had to eat fresh meat. The fat was always trimmed off and that was cooked down for the grease which was used for cooking or making soap," explained Mr. Ben. "When the grease was all cooked out of the pork fat, the little pieces that were left looked about like bits of fried bacon. Those were called cracklings. Some folks mixed those into cornbread batter and baked it. The old chief liked that crackling bread."

Just then David's mother drove up.

"Mom! Mom!" shouted David running to the car. "Can you please wait a little while? Mr. Swain is telling us about the hotel that was there, and the old Indian and he will tell us about the ghost and - - - -."

"Swain?" interrupted Nancy Diven. "Ben Swain?" Nancy got out of the car quickly and looked at the old man in disbelief. "Mr. Ben, is it really you?" she asked.

"Yes, Nancy, it's me, and I'll never forget you and your china dolls."

Nancy held his hand a moment and looked at him, smiling and shaking her head. "Mr. Ben, I thought - - - ."

"No, Nancy, I only went to look after my sister six years ago, but I'm back now living with my son in my old home again."

"Oh, Mr. Ben, this is wonderful. Give me a hug and let me remember so many, many things," said Nancy as tears came into her eyes.

"Thank you, Nancy," said Mr. Ben. "I'm 98 years old and I would live it all over again if I could. Seeing you and visiting here with your David and Corey's Karen, I'm so blessed."

"No, we were blessed, Mr. Ben. There is never a Christmas party or birthday party or school reunion that we don't remember and talk about Mr. Ben," said Nancy.

"Mom, let us get on to the ghost now, please," begged David.

Mr. Ben and Nancy laughed together at the children's excitement and hugged one another again.

"Mom, we need this story for class Monday. This is our homework too!"

"All right, kids, it is a lovely afternoon and I need a few things from the grocery store. Go on with your story and walk Mr. Ben home. I will pick you up there. Karen, I'll call your mother and explain. Later, I'll tell you things about Mr. Ben that I'm sure he won't tell."

"Thanks, Mom.

"Thank you, Mrs. Diven," said Karen.

"Mr. Ben, this is too good to be true. I can't wait to tell Corey." Nancy drove away, delighted that David and Karen were getting to know Mr. Ben.

CHAPTER 3

Getting to Know the Chief

FRIDAY, On the Bench

"Now, where were we?" asked Mr. Ben, as he sat back down and rested both hands atop his cane.

"You told us about the crackling bread. What is jerky?" asked David, as he moved his books to make a seat beside Karen on the sidewalk.

"Jerky is raw meat that has been sliced very thin, then dried in the sun until it is hard and almost black. It is kind of sun-cooked and preserved by being so dry. It will keep a long time that way. Remember we had no refrigeration back then. Chewing jerky was nourishing enough, but I'm not sure you would call it good," explained Mr. Ben, chuckling.

"Is that how Indians fixed their food?" asked Karen.

"You know, I think perhaps we did learn that from the Indians. Now remember, corn and cornbread came from the Indians too. I don't know about the cracklings, but making soap surely came from Europe. The white man's way of preserving meat back then was with salt and smoke, but let's get back to our Indian story," said Mr. Ben.

"Why did he come here?" asked David.

"I asked him that and he said it was to find his grandfather's grave."

"Why here?" asked Karen.

"Because he is buried here, silly," said David.

"Oh! David!" exclaimed Karen in disgust. "I didn't know the Indians ever lived around here."

"Sure they did, long ago," said Mr. Ben.

"How do we know that?" asked David.

"'Cause the chief told him so," replied Karen with a snicker.

"You two stop acting silly," said Mr. Ben, smiling. "Of course, the old chief told us that, but we already knew it because there is lots of evidence that Indians lived here off and on for a long time before we came along to farm and ranch, and build a town."

"Oh, sure," said David. "I have two arrowheads I found by the creek last summer."

"Well, yes, David, but you might find arrowheads anywhere Indians hunted. We know that rock chips and broken and unfinished arrowheads found in the fields just off the road by the creek tell us they camped there. There is a deep hole in the creek and a good all-year spring there, with big trees for shade and firewood. Even today it is a favorite area for deer and other wild animals. I think if I was an Indian I would have camped here, too," explained Mr. Ben.

"Did we build a town here for the same reasons?" asked Karen.

"Yes, I think that is logical," said Mr. Ben. "Then there is another reason. Two trails came together here, one along the river and another that followed the creek off to the north and east. Today our roads, especially the old ones, follow those same routes."

"Why did trails have to follow the creeks and rivers?" asked David.

"It was easier walking along the waterways than going through the hills and woods and, of course, the hunters and travelers wanted to stay close to water. The wild animals stayed close to water also, so hunting was better there."

"Their horses needed water, too," said Karen.

"Yes, but, Karen, you forget, the Indians had no horses before our ancestors came here," said Mr. Ben.

"Oh?" questioned David.

"Indeed," said Mr. Ben, "for most of the long, long history of the Indians, they had no horses and, of course, no cows as we know them. The Spanish explorers brought the first horses and cattle to North America."

"Let's get back to the ghost," begged David.

"Certainly," said Mr. Ben smiling again. "Early every morning the chief rocked in a rocking chair at the end of the upstairs porch of the hotel. Every afternoon he would walk for hours along the creek and back into the brush and hills on the east side of the creek. As he walked along with a long stick in his hand he mumbled a little chant that didn't sound like any words we knew. I recall someone described it as grunts, bumps and wheezes."

"Why did he do that?" asked Karen.

"Well, we might call it superstition, but that would be very unfair and really untrue. It was part of the Indian's religion, and truly, they have a faith uniquely their own. Let's say it was part of his beliefs and culture."

"Well, did he know where to look for his grandfather's grave?" asked David.

"Not exactly," explained Mr. Ben. "He said, 'I will know,' and the way he said it left me believing he would know when he found it."

"Did he find it?" asked Karen.

"Yes, eventually. Late one day in August he came into my store just before closing. He just walked up to me and looked at me. He said nothing, but I could see it in his face. I said, 'You found it?' He just nodded and picked up some peppermint sticks. Oh, I almost forgot to tell you about that. Back then, lemon drops, licorice and peppermint sticks were popular. His favorite was peppermint sticks. They were about as long as your pencil, and red-and-white striped like a barber pole. He bought some every day."

Mr. Ben continued, "Then he held his hands out and apart, which was his way of asking what he owed me. He paid with a twenty-dollar gold piece, but never took any change. I kept a ticket for him and when he had spent it all I would tell him and he would give me another gold piece. He paid his hotel bill the same way."

"But what happened when he found the grave?" interrupted David.

"Well, for days he sat under an old tree just outside the fence of the cemetery up there on Graveyard Hill."

"You mean Boot Hill?" asked David.

"Some call it that," said Mr. Ben. "I asked the chief if his grandfather was buried by that tree and he nodded. 'There where you sit?' I asked. He nodded again. I told him I believed there was something special about that hill that lead us to bury those we love there, too. Chief Longhair looked at me and his eyes were smiling. He nodded again and again, and left."

Mr. Ben sat silent a moment, thinking. "When the chief didn't come out to sit in the rocking chair or for his afternoon walk one day, the hotel clerk went to check on him. He was dead, just lying there straight as an arrow in his bed. No one ever saw the chief really smile, but lying there he seemed to be smiling."

"What did you do?" quizzed Karen.

"We buried him up there by his grandfather. We could find no kin, and nobody even knew his name or where he came from. We dug a grave for the chief there where he sat. Sure enough, we dug up a human bone. We put it back and moved over a little to finish his grave. Folks had taken a liking to the chief, so we moved the cemetery fence over to include his and his grandfather's graves and we put up a little tombstone for each of them."

"That was a kind thing to do," said David.

"I think so, too," said Karen.

"Now, you won't believe this," said Mr. Ben. "I told everyone I would pay the expenses for the old chief's funeral. Well, many folks helped for nothing and we had a nice funeral. We did have to buy a pine coffin and some cement to make the tombstones. When we added up all the bills and used up the credit he had at my store and the hotel, the remaining cost was exactly $20. Now when the hotel cleaned out the chief's room, there under the water pitcher on the nightstand was one last twenty-dollar gold coin."

"Oh my gosh, that is spooky!" exclaimed David.

"Scary is a a better word," said Karen as she shivered a little at the thought.

"Let's start on toward my house, kids," said Mr. Ben. "I was going to tell you some more about the store and hotel and the old chief's ghost, but I just remembered I have a picture of both buildings at home. That will help with the storytelling."

"Oh, yes, I'd like that," said Karen

"Wow, an Indian ghost!" exclaimed David as he gathered up his coat and books.

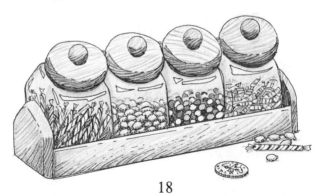

CHAPTER 4

History Turns Spooky

FRIDAY, at Ben Swain's House

As they walked along, Mr. Ben pointed out old landmarks and told of other things that used to be. All these things were interesting, but not as important as the Indian's ghost that the children were so anxious to hear about.

Once the children stopped to giggle at a big bushy tailed squirrel running along the telephone cable between poles across the street.

"I see that squirrel every day about this time," said Mr. Ben. "I enjoy him. Sometimes he comes close just to look at me."

When they reached the Swain house, Mr. Ben invited David and Karen into the living room. He dis-

19

appeared only to return in a moment with another pair of glasses and a framed picture in his hand. He sat down; David and Karen went to look over his shoulder at the picture.

"This old picture was taken before the tornado. The camera was set up upstairs in Dr. Kirbow's house across and down the street a bit from where the school is now. Let's see, the flagpole in the school yard is about here now. This is my first store. You can read my sign even at this angle, and you can see on up Front Street a little way."

"Which was Dr. Kirbow's house?" asked David.

"The real estate company is in that old house now," explained Mr. Ben.

"Oh yes," said Karen, "the one with the big porches; my uncle works there."

"You can see what I meant about the big porches, tall windows, lacy curtains and a sort of spooky look to the old hotel," said Mr. Ben. "Now the chief's room, Room 8, was next to the last room on this side. That was his window right there. You can just see it over that little oak tree."

"Look," said Karen, "there are the lanterns by the front door, too. This is great, Mr. Ben."

"Now, about the ghost?" chided David.

"Well," said Mr. Ben as he sat back a little, "a drummer from St. Louis had a room on the first floor, under the chief's old room. Before the drummer left town, he told me and several others that he had heard someone walking and mumbling in a real peculiar way up there in the chief's room at night. I checked with the hotel clerk and no one had been in any upstairs rooms the night before nor for several days.

"Was there a whole band with the drummer?"

asked Karen.

"Oh no," said Mr. Ben, with a smile, "traveling salesmen were called drummers back then. Let's see, if I remember correctly he was selling shoes, yes, shoes and belts."

"Did anyone else hear the ghost?" asked David.

"Oh, yes," said Mr. Ben, "a lady staying in Room 9, the last one there, said she went into the hall to investigate strange sounds one night and as she passed Room 8, which was empty, a gust of wind blew out her candle. Then she felt the swish of hair as if someone passed her very closely in the dark. As she groped her way back to her room, she smelled peppermint."

Karen shivered at the thought of it.

With eyes wide, David drew in a long slow breath.

"Here at this end of the upstairs porch is where the old chief liked to sit in the big rocking chair and rock at first light every morning," continued Mr. Ben, as he pointed to the porch in the picture. "You can see that chair in the picture. Now Rosco Mullins delivered milk around town about daylight every morning back then. He told everyone that now and then at first light, he would come around the corner, just down from Dr. Kirbow's house, and look up and see that old chair rocking with nobody in it and there was no wind to blow it."

"Wow!" whispered David. "Wait until we tell this to the class."

"Then there was Charley Watkins, another drummer who sold hardware of all kinds. He came to town six or eight times a year. He stayed in Room 8 one night and would never even stay upstairs again. Charley said he never felt alone in that room and he would wake up for no reason at all. Then, at times his hair tickled his head like the wind was blowing it, but there was no wind. Oh yes, he also claimed little things in his room were moved around, and once in the night he smelled peppermint."

"Did everybody who stayed in that room have trouble with the ghost?" asked David.

"No, indeed," said Mr. Ben. "Lots of folks came and went, and for weeks, even months, nothing happened. Then now and again, there would be another story."

"Did anyone ever see the ghost?" asked Karen with a nervous tone to her voice.

"Well, - - - maybe, - - - sort of," said Mr. Ben.

"What do you mean, 'sort of'?" asked David.

"Well - - - ," said Mr. Ben thoughtfully as he looked out of the corners of his eyes, first at David, then across at Karen. "My cousin Dooley Swain stayed there once. We had a big storm with lots of thunder and lightning that night. Dooley swore that now and then flashes of lightning cast faint shadows of an old man with long blowing hair onto the walls of his room. He also said he smelled peppermint plainly once, and his boots and other things were moved in the night. He was in Room 8, of course."

"Did you believe him?" asked David.

"Humph! Some folks did!" said Mr. Ben. "But I'm not so sure. Now old Dooley was quite a character, and he liked to hear himself chatter more than a long-tailed monkey with fleas."

The children laughed.

"Once when my house was being painted, I stayed in the hotel for three nights. I was in Room 7 for two nights and everything was fine. Then, believing I had known the old chief perhaps better than anyone else, I stayed my third and last night in Room 8. Nothing happened. I heard nothing, felt nothing and saw nothing."

"Why?" asked Karen.

"I've always wondered," said Mr. Ben. "Some folks seem to believe in ghosts, and claim to see and hear them. Others just don't believe and have never experienced ghosts."

"Do you believe in ghosts, Mr. Ben?" asked David.

"I'm not sure," said Mr. Ben. "There is no proof. I've never experienced one in my ninety-eight years, but there are some fine, upstanding folks who say 'yes' because they are sure they have seen one or more. I believe it is a matter of personal opinion and we must each decide for ourselves."

"What became of the hotel?" asked David.

"One afternoon in October 1920, a tornado dropped out of a cloud and took the roof and one whole side off my store and the entire upstairs off the hotel. The downstairs of the hotel was left standing, but it and my store were wrecked beyond repair," explained Mr. Ben.

David was holding his breath and staring wide-eyed at the picture again.

"What do you see?" asked Karen.

"Look, look," he said, pointing at the photograph of the little oak tree outside the window of the old chief's room. "See the white rock sticking up out of the ground right by the tree."

"Yes, I see it," said Mr. Ben.

"Yeah," said Karen.

"The big oak tree beside our classroom has a white rock showing between the roots right at the base of the tree."

"Wow! you are right, David. That must be the same tree as in this picture," exclaimed Karen. "That's great."

"It is more than that," said David, as he studied the picture more closely. "If I'm seeing this right, the old chief's room was right where our fourth grade classroom, Room 8, is now."

Karen raced around Mr. Ben's chair to look closely at the picture with David. She began to shiver again. "Oh-h-h! My goshhh!" was all she could say.

Mr. Ben's eyes were wide too. "Hey, kids, that is exciting. Let me look too. Yes, indeed, the high ceilings in the old hotel would make the upstairs about as high as the second floor of your school. Now if that tree is outside your classroom window, you kids just might have a historic ghost in there."

David gulped with fear and then whistled softly.

Karen grimaced and shivered some more.

CHAPTER 5

The Ghost and The Old Photograph

FRIDAY, Going Home

With Corey Murphy standing behind her, Nancy Diven knocked on Ben Swain's front door.

"Come in," invited Mr. Ben.

Nancy came in and Corey stepped around her carrying a potted plant of red geraniums. "A little gift for you, Mr. Ben," she said, as she set the flowers beside the photograph on the coffee table. "Now give me a hug, Mr. Ben."

"Hi, Mom!" said David.

"Hello, Mother," said Karen

"I've seen that picture in your store," said Nancy, picking up the old photograph Mr. Ben had been showing the children.

"Me, too," said Corey.

"That was my first store," explained Mr. Ben. "And the old hotel stood where the school house is now. That is what I'm telling the children about."

"It is a great story, Mom!" said David. "And wait until I tell you and Dad about the old Indian chief and his ghost."

"It's fun, but it's spooky," said Karen. "With all this, we can make our history report Monday. The class is really going to like it."

"Now that we know Mr. Ben is back, we'll see him more!" said Nancy. "That's a promise. I have a potroast cooking, so we need to get on home if you have your story for class."

"One last question, Mom," said David. "Mr. Ben, what happened after the tornado, did anyone see or hear the ghost again?"

"I bought what was left of the store and hotel, and used the lumber to build a larger new store over where the hospital is now. The ghost was forgotten. Years later the new school house was built, and now here you are."

"Where was the old school house?" asked Karen.

"Now, that is a story I can tell," said Corey, "and tonight your Grandma Mitchell will help me tell you about that, and how Mr. Ben became such a legend."

"Oh, great!" said Karen.

"Let's go now," said Nancy. "Give Mr. Ben a hug and thank him for the story."

David and Karen hugged Mr. Ben (to his delight) and thanked him again and again for the wonderful history lesson.

"Why don't you children take the picture to class with you?" said Mr. Ben. "A story without pictures is only half a story at best."

"May we? Oh, thank you so much," said Karen, clapping her hands.

"That would be super!" exclaimed David.

"Then bring it back and tell me how your reports went," said Mr. Ben. "I'm sure you will have more questions by then, and remembering is most of my fun now."

"Thank you, Mr. Ben," said Corey. "We'll come back with the photograph and tell you about the report."

"You aren't the only one who enjoys remembering, Mr. Ben," said Nancy. "Now that these kids know you, we'll have fun, too. Your own story is wonderful to tell also."

As they drove to Karen's house, both mothers began to tell the story of Mr. Ben.

Nancy started, "When the tornado wrecked Mr. Ben's first store, his merchandise was scattered all over this part of town and even in the fields behind the old hotel. The old school was unhurt, but the children rushed out to see what had happened."

"I would have, too," said David.

"Me, too," added Karen.

"Now, Mr. Ben was already popular with children just because he was so friendly. He teased kids in a kind way, and when parents bought an order from his store he always added a surprise or treat for the children."

"He was just like that," said Corey. "It didn't matter if a child was from a poor family that seldom bought much; Mr. Ben always found an excuse to give him or her something, too."

"Mr. Ben wasn't hurt by the tornado, at least, not

badly," said Nancy. "But when children saw him standing there in despair, looking out at his scattered merchandise, one little boy said, 'Don't worry, Mr. Ben, we'll get the things for you!'"

"And they did," said Corey. "All the store merchandise that could be found was picked up and stored in the school house. School was turned out for about a week until Mr. Ben could move all his things to a safe place."

"The children thought that was a nice holiday," said Nancy, "and Mr. Ben found that they had recovered almost all of his merchandise.

"Wow!" exclaimed Karen.

"That's great," said David. "I wish I had been there to help."

"Mr. Ben was so impressed that he made a promise that from then on he would have more things for children than any store in town and every child who was attending school could buy from him at his cost," said Corey.

Nancy giggled. "Yes, he said his only profit from the children would be a hug and their thanks."

"What do you mean by profit, Mom," said David.

"How to explain that - - -" mused his mother. "Let's look at it this way. People who have a job get paid for their work. A merchant's work is to get things that we need, bring them to his store and have them there for us to look over and buy. Now to be fair we must pay him for that work. If he buys something like a towel from a salesman for a dollar then charges us a dollar and twenty-five cents for it, we have paid him twenty-five cents for his work. That twenty-five cents is called his profit."

"Oh, I see," said Karen. "It is the difference between what he paid the drummer and what we pay him."

"Drummer?" snickered Corey. "That's an old term. You kids did listen to Mr. Ben today. That is history and you learned it well. Don't forget to tell about that in class Monday."

"Yes, Mother," said Karen.

"Say, Mom," quizzed David, "last summer we stayed in a motel called 'Drummers Inn.' Is that the kind of drummer they meant?"

"Sure, David," said Nancy, "the name suggests it is a favorite motel for traveling salesmen, so we will think it must be a good one. I believe it is."

David fell back onto the seat in a fit of laughter. "Well, it makes sense now," he said. "I thought it was silly to have a motel for people who played the drums."

Now Karen started giggling, while Nancy and Corey looked at one another half frowning and half smiling.

"You're silly," said Karen, as she pointed at David. He just laughed more at how ridiculous he had been.

Nancy said, "Children, there is a lesson in this. All your life you will find moments when you learn something new or come to understand something that you only guessed at before. Then you will feel silly that you believed something wrong for so long. Fortunately, it is usually something you can laugh about."

"And if you are looking, listening and learning as you have today, life will stay full of wonders and surprises," said Corey.

"Did Mr. Ben keep his promise to the school kids?" asked Karen.

"Yes, he did, for as long as he ran that old store," said Nancy. "If you wanted an item he didn't have, he would get it for you."

"We bought our dolls, doll clothes, skates, jacks and other things from him. The boys got bats and balls, marbles and tops, and all those important things from him, too," explained Corey.

"What happened to his store?" asked David.

"Mr. Ben was already getting old when Nancy and I were in school, David. About the time we went off to high school, he sold his store and retired. Big new stores were being built then. His store building was converted into a small hospital. Later that was torn down to build the big hospital that is there now."

They stopped at Karen's house. "David, how are we going to tell this?" asked Karen.

"Perhaps together?" suggested David. "Do you think Miss Wilson will let us do it that way?"

"I don't know, maybe if we had a plan, an outline

to show her first."

"Okay, I'll call you Saturday and we'll figure out who tells what."

"Sure, but you tell about the ghost. I get too many goose bumps just thinking about it."

"I like that," said David. "What part do you like best?"

"Maybe about the tornado and the school kids and Mr. Ben's promise."

"Sounds okay to me, let's each make a list of things to tell. We'll compare them and make one to follow Monday."

"Okay," said Karen.

"I'll call you about nine o'clock tomorrow morning."

"Bye! It was fun, David!"

"Yeah, Monday will be fun, too, I think."

CHAPTER 6

Show and Tell

FRIDAY NIGHT

The potroast was good, but David was telling about Mr. Ben and the ghost with so much enthusiasm he hardly tasted it. His mom and dad seldom saw David so excited.

"David, I'm enjoying your story," said Tom. "Telling it to us is good practice. This way you will do a better job in class Monday."

"Take a bite of supper now and then," said Nancy, smiling. "I want you strong enough to be able to tell it again Monday. Also, when you stop to chew a little, your memory can catch up to your tongue."

Tom chuckled. "Son, you are doing fine with the story, we're proud of you. You said Mr. Ben loaned you his old photograph and told you it would make telling your story much better. He is right. What else do you have to show?"

"Well, nothing, Dad."

"Let's see, does everyone in your class know where the cemetery, or Boot Hill as you call it, is?"

"I don't know."

"Then you should show them. Let's work on that. Finish your supper while I look for the local map I got from the Chamber of Commerce last summer."

Nancy thought about how David had told the story. "David, I have a suggestion, too. Here and there in your story, you should quote Mr. Ben exactly if you can. It makes your story more colorful and more believable."

"What do you mean by 'quote?'" asked David.

"Let me give you an example," said his mother. "If you were to say 'Mr. Ben told us to show our class this picture because it would make our story better' that would be true, wouldn't it?"

"Yes, Ma'am."

"But if you were to say, 'Mr. Ben insisted we bring this picture to show you and then he said (Nancy changed her voice to mimic Mr. Ben's), 'A story without pictures is only half a story at best.'"

David giggled at Nancy imitating Mr. Ben.

"Now, I quoted Mr. Ben, and the way I did it made it clear that is exactly what he said."

"I see now," said David.

"I was a little silly, and you giggled at it, so I made it colorful and you enjoyed it. Now the class and Miss Wilson will enjoy it too, and they will remember it longer if you will quote Mr. Ben that way now and then."

"Sure, Mom. Let's see, I asked him if he believed his cousin Dooley about seeing the ghost, and he said (David changed his voice to sound like the old man), 'Humph! I'm not so sure. Old Dooley was quite a character, and he liked to hear himself chatter more than a long-tailed monkey with fleas.'"

Nancy laughed so hard David began to laugh too, and Tom came back to see what was happening.

"That was great, David. Tell it that way Monday and yours will be the story of the year," said Nancy as she continued to laugh.

"Okay, Mom, if I can keep from laughing in the middle of it."

"Here is the map, David, but it's too small to show the class. Can you use the chalkboard to tell your story?" asked Tom.

"I think so."

"Get a scratch pad and we'll work out what you should draw on the chalkboard."

David returned with pad and pencil, and they sat down to study the map.

"Now, David, of course you already know that on all regular maps the top side is north, so the right side is east. Front Street is parallel to the river and runs north and south. Draw a line from the top to the bottom of the chalkboard. Now draw the river on the left like this; make it a little crooked like the river and use the chalk flat to make it wide."

"Oh, sure," said David.

"Now, Cherry Street crosses Front Street by the school like this."

"Yeah."

"Put in just a few more streets; that is enough. Now let's put in the school, and the hospital and Dr. Kirbow's old house, and Mr. Ben's house right here. Oh, yes, even the Murphy's house way over here."

"Sure, why not? Karen will like that," said David.

"Our house is too far out to put on this map. We are way on out this way. Now the creek goes off away from the river up here about like this. So, here is the road by the creek and then this one is Cemetery Road. It goes back to the east. Right about here is the cemetery, and if my memory is correct, the tree with the Indians' graves is about there."

"Oh, great, Dad. I found my arrowheads over here by the creek, didn't I?"

"Yes, David, that is right. Now if you draw a map or two, you will learn more about how to read maps. That is important. Can you find all this on the little map too?"

"Let's see, here is the river and there is the creek, so this must be Front Street, yes, here is the name. Now where is Cherry Street? Here. No, that is Ash. Oh! That must be the school," said David.

"Correct. Now, the old Indian searched east of the creek in the woods and hills for his grandfather's grave. Where would that be?"

"East, that is the right side on the map, so it was out here. Oh sure, and Boot Hill is east of the creek too."

"Right! Now where is the corner Rosco Mullins turned when he said he could see the empty chair rocking?"

"That would be about here."

"No, wrong side of the school. Remember you said it was just past Dr. Kirbow's house, that is south, here. And where did Mr. Ben say the chair was?"

"Here on the upstairs porch of the hotel. Mr. Mullins had to come this way to see it. Where was the old school, Dad?"

"Here next to the hospital and almost across the street from Mr. Ben's first store. The tornado must have scattered his things out this way right behind the old hotel. That used to be fields. It is full of houses now."

"Okay, Dad."

"That is enough streets and landmarks to tell your story, David. Any more would take too much time and be confusing. Now watch me draw this. All maps have a north arrow, a straight line with a big capital "N".

Tom tore the page off the scratch pad and folded it up. "Now, David, you draw all that again and this time put names on the river, the creek and Front and Cherry Streets like on the little map. If you explain your map as you draw it on the chalkboard your class will understand it."

"Okay, Dad, north is up here and Front Street runs north and south like this. Then Cherry Street goes this way - - - "

CHAPTER 7

Grandma Mitchell Remembers the Ghost

As the Murphys were finishing supper, Karen began telling of the visit with Mr. Ben.

"Grandma, Mother said you would tell me about the old school and more about Mr. Ben."

"Yes, Karen, like Mr. Ben, I enjoy talking about the past. Let me tell you first about the old school and another thing about Mr. Ben. Then, I remember a couple of things about the Indian chief and his ghost I'm sure you will want to know."

"Oh, great!" said Karen. "Wow! David will love that too."

Grandma Mitchell's eyes sparkled at Karen's excitement. "I'm glad to see you have found delight in discovering the past, Karen. Imagining the future is the other thrill you will enjoy too."

"Yes thanks, Grandma. Now tell me about the school and the ghost."

"Of course. Karen, your great-great-grandfather Andrew Mitchell and several of his neighbors built that old school. It was very small and stood where the little park is now, there beside the hospital."

"Oh, I know where that is," said Karen.

"At first it was just one room with a big wood-burning stove in one corner. The teachers and students had to keep the fire going in the winter time. Later another room was added and then two more. As the town grew the school always seemed to be too small. After the tornado, plans were made to build a large new school where the old hotel had been. Some years later we built it and now you go to school there."

"Where was the high school, Grandma?"

"Well, that building was both elementary school and high school back then. Now it is only elementary school, and there are two more schools," said Corey, "both a middle school and a high school."

"Now Karen, you mentioned crackling bread, and other things Grandma can tell you more about," said John. "One more thing about Mr. Ben; he was known for something more than the things he did for kids."

"Yes, indeed," said Grandma Mitchell, "he kept a closet for the needy or anyone in trouble, such as after a fire or tornado. Everyone gave things to Mr. Ben's closet, and somehow he always had what was needed to give to anyone who really needed help. There was no Red Cross nor Salvation Army nor welfare back then. We only had Mr. Ben's closet and everyone was proud of it."

"No wonder everyone loved Mr. Ben. Tell me

about making soap, Grandma."

"I'm not sure Corey ever saw any of us make soap, Karen. My mother made it when I was a girl and I still made some before your mother was born."

"I only remember my mother buying Octagon Soap at Mr. Ben's, and bars of hand soap that had colored streaks in them like marbles," said Corey.

"Oh my, yes, Corey. Octagon Soap was a little like homemade soap, but much better. I don't recall the brand of the old hand soap."

"How did you make homemade soap, Grandma?"

"We cooked fat down for the grease. If it was pork fat, we called the grease 'lard' and we cooked with it like we do with shortening and vegetable oils now."

"Did you use the crackling, Grandma?"

"Oh, sure. We made crackling bread too. I suspect the chief ate some of ours because we often traded bread to Mr. Ben for other things."

"Oh, this is fantastic," exclaimed Karen.

"Now when we cooked down beef fat, we used the grease, which is called tallow, for soap. When we saved up enough, we put it in a big iron kettle out in the yard and built a fire under it."

"Like a witch's brew?" asked Karen.

"Well yes," said Grandma Mitchell with a smile. "First we boiled the tallow with water in it and let it cool. The fat would float to the top, clean and white. We dipped this off carefully into buckets, cleaned out the pot, and put the clean tallow back into it."

"Is that all?"

"Oh no, we've just started," said Grandma Mitchell. "We added lye and borax, which we bought at Mr. Ben's store, then put in some clean water and stirred it awhile."

"Did you build a fire under it again?" asked Karen.

"No, when the lye and water mix, it gets very hot all by itself."

"How did you know how much of each to use, Grandma?" asked Corey.

"The recipe for good soap was always on the label on the cans of lye. We stirred this until it was nice and creamy, and would stay that way. Then we put it in big flat pans where it cooled and hardened into soap. Before it got too hard, we cut it into bar-size pieces with a knife."

"Like we cut up brownies right out of the oven?" asked Karen.

"Yes, indeed," chuckled Grandma, "only the pieces were larger."

"Sure," said Karen beaming. "That is a good story too. I'll have fun telling how homemade soap is made like a Halloween witch's brew in a big black iron pot. How do you spell lye and borax, Mother?"

"L-Y-E and B-O-R-A-X."

"Do you need to show the class the size and shape of the big kettle?" asked John.

"Well, yes, how big was it, Dad?"

John held out his arms in a big circle and explained the round bottom.

"Mom, is that like the big kettle we used to bob for apples in the backyard at Sandy Barton's house last Halloween?"

"Of course, Karen, good thinking."

"Now I remember Sandy's mother said it was her grandmother's old pot and it was used for washing and making soap," said Karen. "How did they wash in it?"

"We boiled very dirty clothes in it with some of the soap we made," said Grandma. "That was usually the men's and boys' work clothes, and the aprons and things we used when handling fresh meat."

"How did you wash the regular clothes, Grandma?"

"In a tub, by hand on a scrub board," said Grandma. "We didn't have any washing machines then. Even the first machines were cranked by hand."

"Washing sure was a lot of work back then," said Karen.

"Everything was a lot of work back then," said John. "We forget, or perhaps kids your age just don't know, how much things have changed in just two or three generations."

Grandma smiled and nodded her head. "Karen, I am eighty-two years old and when I was your age we had only one car. It was a noisy, smoky, open-top contraption and the driver had to start it with a crank. We had no electricity for lights, so there were no refrigerators nor washing machines, radios nor television and only a few hand-cranked telephones."

"Mr. Ben told us some about that, too."

"There was no air-conditioning then either," said John."They couldn't heat or cool the house by adjusting the thermostat."

"Were people miserable then, Grandma?"

"No indeed, Karen," said Grandma. "Some say we worked harder back then, but not really. Perhaps longer and certainly at different things than now. We were happy. I wouldn't want to live that way again because, like you, I am used to all the modern things now."

"Karen," said John, "we look back and marvel at how much we have changed the way we live in about one hundred years and that is fascinating. Then when we stop to think that every thing continues to change and one day when you are Grandma's age your grandkids will say, 'Grandma Karen, you sure did live in hard times. Were you miserable?' What will you tell them?"

"No, Dad, I'm happy."

"Grandma, you promised to tell us more about the chief and his ghost," said John.

"Please do," said Karen.

"Oh my, yes," said Grandma Mitchell. "The chief seemed to love children. Often he would stop by the school to watch them or when he saw them playing in yards or on the street. He never said anything but seemed to watch with a certain contentment. The children said he was stonefaced, but his eyes were gentle and smiling."

"He never said anything?" asked Karen.

"No, but when the children waved to him he always waved back by touching his heart with his hand and waving ever so gently like this." Grandma Mitchell touched her heart and waved her open hand slowly as she held it high.

"Why did he do that?" asked Karen.

"Just his way," said Grandma. "Kids thought it was the friendliest wave they ever saw. When they waved back the same way he would nod pleasantly. Children loved it, and then often waved to their friends the same way. To them, it became something very special."

"Oh, this is great. Thanks, Grandma. Now about the ghost?"

"I knew the lady in Room 9 in the hotel that Mr. Ben told you about. She was my friend's aunt. She said she sometimes heard things at night too and when she asked, she was told about the chief. She stayed there a while, but was never afraid. She was convinced there was a ghost, but a friendly one."

"Is there more?" asked Karen.

"No," said Grandma. "Everything else I recall Mr. Ben has already told you."

Karen gave Grandma a hug and a kiss, and thanked her for the story.

"It's getting late, Karen. Now about Monday. Are you ready?" asked her father.

"My arithmetic is done, Dad, and I'll read my science when I get to bed."

"That's a good girl, Karen. Holler if you need some help."

"Thanks. Oh, may I call David first and tell him

what I just learned?

"Yes, Karen, of course, he will want to know."

"Super," exclaimed Karen as she hurried to the telephone.

"Granny," said John, "Mr. Ben is right. Pictures or anything to show makes a story better. Don't we have some pictures of the old farm in the family album?"

"Yes, John, yes. There were some of Great-grandpa and Uncle Joe and Mr. Warren butchering a steer. I believe the old kettle was cooking right there in the picture."

"Those are in the bookcase upstairs," said Corey. "I'll get them and Grandma can tell Karen about them. She can use them for class, too."

"School was never quite like this when I was young." said Grandma with a sigh. "It would be fun to be a kid again now."

"You're right, Granny," said John. "But let me tell you, every night's homework isn't a ghost story to tell and a fun visit with Grandma. Some nights Karen works hard on her lessons. School doesn't let kids off with just letters and numbers practiced on one little slate anymore."

"Some nights we work as hard as she does just helping her," said Corey. "I believe parents should get a diploma when their kids graduate."

Grandma smiled. "Are you and John learning something, too, Corey?"

"You bet we are, Grandma," said Corey.

"Granny," said John, as he cocked his head seriously, "I'm convinced that parents have a second chance at a good basic education if they will just help their children with their homework."

"Oh, I know that, John," said Grandma smugly.

"I'm glad and proud that both of you have learned the truth. Corey, your grandfather and I didn't get a whole lot of education in the old school. We learned the most helping you and Mike with your homework. Remember?"

"I remember you both helped us. You even reviewed our class-work. I didn't know you were learning too."

"We sure were."

"Well, I'll be a long-haired Barbie doll," said Corey.

"You were, and a Valedictorian too," said Grandma smugly.

CHAPTER 8

A Challenge from Chester

MONDAY MORNING

Karen joined Miss Wilson as she walked from the street corner to the school. Chester White was a few steps behind them.

Miss Wilson, for class today, may David and I do our reports together?"

"That is unusual. Why together, Karen?"

"It just happened that we got our information together, and it is long enough to divide between us."

"What is it about, Karen?"

"The schoolhouse and what used to be here, Miss Wilson."

"Oh boy," exclaimed Chester acidly, "just what we need to know more about, this old schoolhouse."

"Hush, Chester," chided Miss Wilson.

"There is more about making jerky and soap - - - "

"Aa-a-a—gh," groaned Chester.

"But that is for a later report," continued Karen.

"How do you propose to divide it between you, Karen?" asked Miss Wilson as they started up to the second floor.

Chester decided to wait by the front door. He had a smirk on his face.

"We made this outline."

"Let me see. Oh! Oh yes, I see." She stopped short and looked at Karen. "This ghost part, now that must be something. Are you two sure about this, Karen?"

"Here is a note from my mother about the report. She said you would want some explanation."

"Yes, I would. Hmmm-mm-m."

"Is it okay, Miss Wilson?"

"Well, all right. Yes, I like your plans to take turns telling the story, that should be interesting. We will try it, Karen."

"Thank you."

"I'll look forward to this one, Karen. It should be exciting."

"Don't tell anyone, Miss Wilson, please don't tell."

"Of course not, Karen. That would spoil the fun, wouldn't it? But thank you for the preview, at least I should be prepared."

"Thank you, ma'am."

David hurried up the walk toward the door. Chester White leaned against the wall with his foot propped up. He was looking smart-faced.

"This is your day, Champ," chided Chester. "Boy, I just can't wait to be told about this old schoolhouse. Here, here, sir." He held out his hand. "Would you be

47

so kind as to show me the way to my room? This is only my fourth year here; I still get lost in the wonders of this grand old place."

"Stick your hand and your head in your pocket, Creep," responded David.

"Sir," continued Chester in a high voice, "the girls are holding their breath to learn about jerky and soap. My, my, how can we go on without knowing about that?"

"Just go away," said David, as he started upstairs with Chester on his heels.

"Oh sir, your wonderful lectures just thrill me to the bottom of my little old heart," continued Chester. "I just haven't been the same since you told us about the bugs and worms."

"Gypsy moths, Chester, now drop dead."

They entered the room with Chester still dogging David. "My, my, yes, it was gypsy moths," he continued in his taunting high voice. "Are they threatening to devour this darling old schoolhouse, sir?"

Miss Wilson observed Chester's last heckle. "Chester!" she said sternly.

"Yes, Ma'am?"

"You are in fine voice today. Would you like to give your report this afternoon?"

"Oh, no, ma'am!"

"Then I trust I have heard the very last of your foolishness for today. Understood?"

Chester nodded sheepishly.

The day progressed with no unusual events, except that Chester drew a picture of a large worm eating the schoolhouse and taunted David with it in English class. After lunch it was a large moth consuming the building. Some of the class laughed. David didn't.

At noon David and Karen went over their outline together one more time. Karen showed David the pictures of the old kettle at her grandmother's house. They agreed again that Karen would tell the soap-making story for her next report.

David prepared the chalkboard for his map.

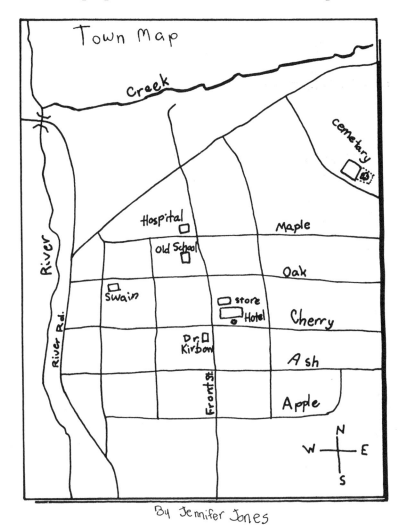

By Jennifer Jones

CHAPTER 9

History Gets Exciting

MONDAY AFTERNOON

As the social studies class began, David took his seat in the second row. Karen, as usual, sat near the windows.

Miss Wilson looked over the room and said, "Today David and Karen are scheduled for reports. This will be unusual since they will take turns telling a story they researched together. Their outline excites my imagination. I'll tell you no more. David, you may begin."

David headed for the chalkboard as Miss Wilson took a seat in the back of the room. Chester half-muffled a wheezing snicker.

David picked up the chalk and took a nervous deep

breath. He stole a quick look at Karen and Miss Wilson. Karen held up her crossed fingers and Miss Wilson gave David her usual smile and nod that plainly said, "Come on, I'm rooting for you."

"We all know that all regular maps show north at the top and that makes east on the right. Front Street goes north and south, so this is Front Street. Now the river - - - - - "

David drew his map with the explanations his dad taught him. "Now, this is the school here at the corner of Front and Cherry. Our story starts on this bench across the street last Friday after school. Karen?"

Karen went to the front of the room and put the outline on Miss Wilson's desk where she and David could both refer to it. "David and I walked out of school last Friday worrying about today's report. There on the bench sat a friendly old man named Mr. Ben Swain. He had lost the lens out of his glasses and - - "

Karen told about their conversation with Mr. Ben. "And Mr. Ben said, 'Do you want to hear about the old store and hotel that were right here where the school is now, or about the tornado, or the Indian chief and his ghost?'"

There were a few gasps and shuffling as the students sat up in their seats. Even Chester White sat up and the smirk began to fade from his face. "Of course, we said, 'All of those things, please.' We will tell you that story today. Now, Mr. Ben said a story without pictures is only half a story at best, so David drew the map we need and we have a very old photograph that is real important to this story. David?"

David erased the school house from the map and drew in the old hotel and Mr. Ben's first store. He also drew in the old school and explained how Karen's great-great-grandfather helped build it. "The old Travelers' Hotel and Mr. Ben's first store were here. This picture of both buildings was taken in 1912 from the upstairs window of Dr. Kirbow's house which is now the real estate company here on the map. The date is on the picture."

David held up the photograph for the class to see. "Notice the porches on the front of the hotel. The facade of Mr. Ben's store, that means this big front, faced on Front Street as all the stores in town did then. That is why they named it Front Street."

"Excellent, David, tell us more," said Miss Wilson.

"Now one day in the spring of 1915, an old man signed into the old Travelers' Hotel with an 'X.' Mr. Ben says back then - - "

David quickly told about Mr. Ben's observations and comments about education in the old days. "Mr. Ben said no one could understand the old Indian's name so they called him, 'Chief' or 'Chief Longhair.' He didn't say much at all, but he looked at you real friendly like he could read your mind. Anyway, folks around town came to like him. Karen?"

Karen went to the front of the room while David stood to the side. "The chief would only eat stew and barbecue at the hotel. He liked jerky and crackling bread which he bought at Mr. Ben's store. Oh, yes, he liked peppermint candy, too. Most every day he bought peppermint sticks about this long, and red-and-white striped like a barber pole. I'll tell about the jerky, crackling bread and homemade soap in my next history report. We don't have time today."

"Fine, Karen," said Miss Wilson.

"My great-grandmother, Grandma Mitchell, told

me the chief liked children," continued Karen. As she explained about his watching and waving to them, she demonstrated how he had waved. When she told how the children began waving to their friends that way, the class waved back to her with the same touch to the heart and hand held high. This made her feel good, for they all thought the chief's wave contained some friendly magic.

"Sometimes the chief cooked rabbits over a fire behind the hotel. Since he had no gun nor bow and arrows, no one knew how he got the rabbits. That was strange."

The class was now paying very close attention.

"The chief rocked in a chair at the end of the upstairs porch very early every morning. Then he walked around in the woods and hills every afternoon, mumbling a chant and searching. When Mr. Ben asked him what he was looking for, he replied, 'my grandfather's grave.'"

The class was attentive and listening carefully now.

"One more spooky thing, the old chief paid Mr.

Ben and the hotel with twenty-dollar gold coins, but he wouldn't take any change. They kept a record of the change for him and when he had spent it all, he gave them another gold coin. Now, back to David."

David went to the chalkboard. "The chief walked mostly in the area east of the creek for weeks and weeks. Then he began to sit under the same tree every day just outside the cemetery. Finally, he came into Mr. Ben's store one day and just stared at Mr. Ben with a satisfied look in his eyes. Mr. Ben said, 'You found your grandfather's grave?' The chief nodded. Mr. Ben asked, 'Is it there where you sit under the tree?' The chief nodded again.

David paused, his self-confidence was growing rapidly. The class was on the edge of their seats. Chester's mouth was open. "Now, this is weird," said David, as he began to get the feel of the story and put more emotion into his voice. He leaned over and gestured with his hands, looking first this way, then that. "Mr. Ben said to the chief, 'That hill must be very special because we bury our folks out there, too.' The chief nodded and nodded, and almost smiled. He never ever really smiled."

"Not at all?" asked Viki Cantu softly.

"Not at all," said David just as softly. "Now this is even spookier. One day the chief didn't come out to his rocking chair, nor for his walk, nor to sit under the tree. When the hotel clerk went to check on him, the clerk found the chief in his bed, dead. Mr. Ben said he was just there, straight as an arrow, unscratched, and finally sorta smiling."

Several deep breaths and low moans filled the class room.

"Karen, your turn."

David's growing confidence began to influence Karen, too. A wink from Miss Wilson encouraged her more. She copied David's developing style by showing emotion, gesturing with her hands and her eyes, speaking softly and mysteriously.

"The townspeople never found any kin for the chief, so lots of folks helped with the funeral. They started digging a grave for the old chief under his tree, and sure enough they found human bones. So they moved over and buried him beside his grandfather."

Karen pointed to the tree by the graveyard on David's map. "They moved the graveyard fence over so the Indians would be inside the cemetery with all the other graves."

The quiet students gave soft Oh's and Ah's.

"Tombstones were placed over both graves. Now this is real weird again. When Mr. Ben added up the cost of the coffin and the grave markers, and used up all the chief's credit at his store and the hotel, there was exactly twenty dollars still owed. They cleaned out the chief's room and found one last twenty-dollar gold coin under the water pitcher on the dresser."

"Wow," said Hector Garza, "that is spooky."

The class just looked at one another and mumbled softly.

CHAPTER 10

Comes the Ghost

MONDAY - History Class
The report continues

"Your turn, David."

David looked at the interested faces of his class-mates. Even Miss Wilson looked anxious to hear more, but it was Chester's frozen features that motivated David most. David pointed out across the class silently for one dramatic moment. "Now this will really give you the willies. There was a drummer from St. Louis staying in a room downstairs right under the chief's room. One night he heard someone walking around up there and mumbling in a peculiar way. When they checked, there was nobody staying upstairs right then."

Chester began to slide down in his seat. Eddie Vickers whistled softly and Trisha Warren said, "Ooo-oo-o" through chattering teeth.

"You mean a drummer from a band, David?" interrupted Miss Wilson.

"No, that is what they called traveling salesmen in those days. Now, the old chief's room was Room 8, and one time a lady staying in Room 9 heard strange sounds. She went into the hall with a lighted candle to investigate. They had no electric lights back then. As she passed Room 8, a sudden gust of wind blew out her candle, but there was nobody in Room 8. Just then she felt the swish of hair as if someone with long hair passed her in the dark, and as she groped her way back to her room, she smelled peppermint."

David paused a moment. Kelly O'Brien who sat behind Chester leaned over and blew gently on the back of Chester's neck. Chester quivered a little and muffled a groan. Miss Wilson tapped Kelly on the shoulder and shook her finger at him.

David smiled. "Karen's Grandma Mitchell knew that lady and heard her tell more about the ghost. The lady was never afraid, although she knew there was a ghost, because she was sure he was friendly and made her feel comfortable."

"Did the lady leave the hotel then?" interrupted Trisha.

"No, she stayed on," said David.

"Why not, if you are not afraid?" added Kelly, as he poked Chester's back with his finger.

David continued. "A hardware drummer, who came to town regularly, stayed in Room 8 one night. He said he kept waking up for no reason and his hair tickled his head like the wind was blowing it, but

58

there was no wind. Also, he said he never felt alone, and little things around his room kept getting moved. And he said once in the night he even smelled peppermint."

Chester rubbed the back of his neck. Kelly was about to break into open laughter when Miss Wilson cleared her throat rather firmly.

"Back then a man named Rosco Mullins delivered milk around town at the crack of dawn every morning. He told that now and then he would come around this corner, past Dr. Kirbow's house real early and look up here and see the chair the old chief rocked in every morning just-a-rocking, with no one in it and no wind to blow it."

There wasn't a sound. David was enjoying the attention of the class. Only Karen flicked a little smile at him.

"Mr. Ben had a cousin named Dooley Swain. Now Dooley Swain stayed in Room 8 one very stormy night just a few months after Chief Longhair died. Dooley said when he woke to the thunder and lightning, some flashes cast a dim shadow of an old man with long hair onto the walls of his room. Dooley began to smell peppermint real plain. And he went on to say his boots and other things were all there next morning, but not where he put 'em."

By now David was talking in a loud whisper for effect. Another smile and wink from Miss Wilson encouraged him to continue the drama. The class sat motionless.

"Later Mr. Ben stayed at the hotel three nights while his house was being painted. He was in Room 7 for two nights and everything was fine." David continued to speak in his suspenseful whisper. "Then

Mr. Ben decided that since he had known the chief better than anyone he would stay his third and last night in Room 8. Well - - - - - guess what?"

David broke into his regular voice with a big smile, and held his arms up. "Nothing. Mr. Ben didn't see, hear or smell a thing."

Suddenly with deep breaths, sighs and smiles, the class relaxed.

David continued, "I asked Mr. Ben if he believed what his cousin Dooley had said about the ghost." David wobbled his head and made a comic face, then broke into his best mimicking voice. "And he said, 'Humph! Some folks did, but I'm not so sure. Old Dooley was a lovable character, but he liked to hear himself chatter more than a long-tailed monkey with fleas.'"

Everyone exploded into laughter. The emotional release was so sudden other teachers came down the hall to look into the fourth grade room and see what was happening. Miss Wilson had to wave them away because she couldn't stop laughing long enough to explain.

"Your turn, Karen," said David.

Karen tried to talk, but had to stop to regain her composure.

"Move on quickly, Karen," said Miss Wilson. "It's getting late."

"Yes, ma'am," said Karen. "One afternoon in October 1920, a tornado dropped out of a cloud and destroyed Mr. Ben's store and the hotel. No one was hurt bad, but Mr. Ben's merchandise was scattered all over the place. At that time, there were fields out behind the hotel and lots of Mr. Ben's stuff was all out there."

Karen went to the map and pointed out the area. "The kids in the school all loved Mr. Ben. School turned out so the kids could help him get all his things picked up. They put everything in the school house for a while, and there was no school until Mr. Ben moved it all."

"Hey! Hey!" said Scott McCoy, "nice way to get a holiday, huh!"

The class all laughed.

"Hush," said Miss Wilson. "Go on, Karen."

"For that, Mr. Ben promised he would have more things in his new store for kids than any other store, and kids in school could always buy them at his cost," continued Karen. "His only profit was a hug now and then, and their thanks of course.

"Oh, that was nice," said Miss Wilson.

"His old store and the old hotel were torn down, and then a few years later this school building was built right here." Karen went to the chalkboard and erased the store and hotel, and drew the school back again.

"Okay, back to David," she said.

David went to the chalkboard and picked up the chalk, then turned and smiled at the class. "Mr. Ben said ghosts seem to occur only when people know about them and are sensitive to them. Well, Karen and I just told you about the old chief. Now let me show you one more thing."

"Hurry, David, we are almost out of time," said Miss Wilson.

"Yes, ma'am," replied David. "On this map, this class room is about right here in the school." David could feel the class getting tense. Suddenly everyone was very still and silent again. "Look at this old photograph again. The old chief's room where he died, and the ghost walked and things, was Room 8, the next to the last window, right there." He pointed to the spot.

Everyone, even Miss Wilson, was leaning forward to look at the old picture. "See that little oak tree right by the window and the white rock sticking out of the ground beside it," continued David with a note of authority. "Now look out our window," he said dramatically, pointing to the windows. "That big oak tree, as you all know has a white rock between its roots up next to the trunk." Everyone was staring at the tree. "That, my friends, is the same tree." He waited a moment until everyone turned to look at him again. In his best mysterious voice, he said, "That means the old chief's room, Room 8, the haunted room, was right here where our classroom, also Room 8, is now. - - - That is all we have to say."

No one moved. There was a frozen moment. Into that tense silence, the bell rang.

Chester turned his desk over jumping out of it.

Miss Wilson was hard pressed to restore order and get Chester back in his seat. "Annie and Stephen, don't forget to have your reports ready tomorrow, if you can get over this one." She smiled. "And have a good evening, class."

There wasn't much talk as the students gathered their things and started down the stairs. Chester was unusually quiet. David came up behind him and flicked the hair on the back of his head and said, "Boo!"

Chester jumped, but made no response. He looked at David a moment in grim silence, and then hurried out of the room.

"David and Karen, that report was well done and very dramatic; perhaps too dramatic. I hope your ghost doesn't haunt us into a problem here," said Miss Wilson.

Karen giggled. David smiled.

"Your report will be a memorable one. Wait until I tell the other teachers about it. Can we keep the photograph here a few days? I think all the teachers and the principal will want to see it and hear about all of this. I'll take good care of it."

"I'll call Mr. Ben and explain," said David.

"Thank you. - - - Wow! I'm the only teacher with a haunted classroom. Well, - - - - - - maybe!"

CHAPTER 11

The Mystery Begins

MONDAY After School

David and Karen went downstairs feeling much better than they had the Friday before. They were both deep in thought as they reached the bench across the street.

David sat down with his books on his lap. "I believe we did okay, Karen."

"Sure! I think we'll get a good grade on it. Miss Wilson seemed to like it."

"You don't think the ghost will give us trouble, do you?" asked David.

"I don't know. It is awfully spooky. Did you plan to get so dramatic?"

"No, it just sorta happened. Did I get carried away?"

"Yes, - - - - some," said Karen.

"Well, you did, too, at the end."

"Everyone liked it though. A few were really scared."

"Chester was especially scared, but he deserved it."

"Hey, look, there is the squirrel again," said David pointing overhead at the telephone cable.

The squirrel stopped to look down at them, and flipped his bushy tail. Both children laughed as the squirrel peeked over one side of the telephone cable, then over the other side. Finally he raced on to the corner and perched atop the pole to rest.

"It was fun, David. See you tomorrow," said Karen as she started on home.

When Karen got to the corner, she turned to see David smiling at her. She touched her heart and waved the chief's wave. David returned the special wave. They both felt the magic of this friendly greeting.

Nancy drove up and David climbed into the backseat.

As he began to buckle his seat belt, he said, "The report went fine, Mom. Maybe we scared some kids, but Miss Wilson liked it. She asked us to leave Mr. Ben's old photograph for her to show to the other teachers."

"We must call Mr. Ben, David."

"Yes, Mom, soon as I get home. Mom, I forgot to show you my arithmetic test paper Friday."

"I found it in your room this morning, David. It's wonderful! I'm proud of it and I called Mr. Dean. He said the puppies will be old enough to leave their mother week after next. One is for you and I'm to call him Monday of that week."

"Great, Mom, I like the one with two white front feet."

"I know. I believe he picked you out, too. He followed you all the way to the car that day."

"Yeah, and he tugged on my pants' leg, too."

"Tonight we'll show your father your test paper. He will be proud. We will want to hear about your report, too. Oh yes, I suggest you ask your father to help you get ready for the puppy."

"Get ready?" asked David. "I'm ready now, Mom."

"Oh, no. You will need a bed inside and a doghouse for him outside. And then you better check the backyard fence so he can't get out and get lost or hurt. You will need dogfood, and feed and water bowls, even a collar. Perhaps you should talk to the vet about shots for the puppy and how to control fleas. Have you thought of a name for him yet?"

"My gosh, Mom. I didn't know a puppy was so complicated."

"Even a puppy requires doing your homework, David. Tomorrow afternoon we'll go by the library and find a book or two on dogs. Okay?"

"Yeah, Mom. Maybe I could make my next report on raising a puppy."

"A lot has changed just in my lifetime, David. You could make a good report on that and you would be ready for your puppy, too."

"Great, Mom," said David. "Could I ask Mr. Ben about it?"

"He would like that, David."

CHAPTER 12

Haunting Happenings

TUESDAY

In social studies class, Annie reported on the history of the local pecan orchards. She had bags of many varieties of pecans, and gave samples of all the pecans to everyone in the class. She used David's map that was still on the chalkboard to explain that pecan trees grow in deep soil, and in the river and creek flood-plains. She showed that most of the town had a rocky base, little topsoil and few pecan trees.

Steven had taken pictures of many old houses to show how homes got bigger and better as the town got older. "This old house was built by my great-uncle over a hundred years ago. My first picture of it was not very good because I am just learning to use my new camera. Dad drove me out to the old house again yesterday. We stopped at the cemetery and took pictures of the Indians' grave stones that Karen told about yesterday."

"Excellent, Steven," said Miss Wilson.

"Oh, great! Thanks," said Karen.

"Wow! Show us," said David.

"I took three pictures. This one shows the tree and graves from over by the gate. Then I took pictures close up of each tombstone. I forgot to refocus my camera on the grandfather's grave, so it is just a fuzzy blur. You can see the shape, but you can't read it. See."

"But the chief's marker is a good picture," said David.

"How did you get these so quickly?" asked Miss Wilson.

"We took them to the new one-hour film service in the Mall," said Steven.

"That was thoughtful, Steven," said Miss Wilson. "This keeps our local history reports current and interesting."

"Thank you, Annie and Steven. These were good reports today. I want to commend all of you for showing as much as you tell. Oh, yes, speaking of showing, I have news. The school is being wired for television sets in each room. We will be able to see lots of things from both tapes and current news."

The boys and girls were excited. "Where will we put the television set, Miss Wilson?" asked Annie.

"Right up here on this front storage cabinet," she said. "Some work has already been done." She pointed to the big picture of George Washington that leaned against the wall on top of the storage cabinet.

"It will be up here where all of you can see it. We'll find a new place for the picture. Now, we are out of time. Remember the history report schedule posted here on the bulletin board. Let's see, tomorrow we hear from Viki and Kevin."

The bell rang.

Spooks and Nuts

WEDNESDAY

Midmorning in English Class, as Miss Wilson opened the storage cabinet for supplies, she looked on top and frowned. "Children, who took the pecans I left on top of this cabinet yesterday?"

There was no answer. She put her hands on her hips and looked sternly at the class.

"The ghost must have gotten them," said Sandy Barton with a laugh.

The class responded with giggles, chuckles and smiles.

"Don't be silly! I want an answer."

"Miss Wilson, I see one under your desk and another in the corner behind the waste basket."

"Yes, you're right, Sandy. Thanks, but there were more."

"How about behind the cabinet, Miss Wilson?" said Kim Koy.

"Not much room there. Yes, I see a small one. Well, something sure scattered them. This still isn't all. There were lots more."

The bell rang.

A Cluttered Classroom

THURSDAY

Miss Wilson, as usual, was the first to go upstairs to her classroom. She was surprised to find a few pencils and other small items from the students' desks scattered about on the floor. This was unusual. The scattered and lost pecans came back to her mind. For the moment she was uncomfortable with her thoughts. She put her purse and papers on her desk and started to pick up the items from the floor.

"Good morning, Miss Wilson," said David as he strolled into the room and headed for his desk. "I'll help you pick up those things. What happened?"

"I don't know. I just got here, David."

Kim Koy came into the room in time to hear David's question and Miss Wilson's answer. She said nothing, but helped pick up two pencils. As Kim handed them to the teacher, she said, "I don't understand. Has anyone been here since yesterday?"

Miss Wilson saw the expression on Kim's face. "I don't think so, Kim." She paused. "It wasn't a ghost," she continued with firm assurance.

The students entering the room heard Miss Wilson's statement to Kim. No fourth grader could leave this alone for long. At recess and lunch, whispers and giggles grew into more open conversation. After lunch, someone just had to ask.

"Miss Wilson," asked Viki. "What happened this morning and what about a ghost?"

"Relax, children. The report made by David and Karen has your imaginations turned on. Yes, some things from your desks were on the floor this morning. True, that was unusual, but that does not indicate there is a ghost. Look, this is an old school. Many, many classes have gone through here for lots of years. There has never been a ghost before, so logically, there is not one now."

"Yes, ma'am," said Viki.

"Anyway," said Miss Wilson, with her most sure and authoritative voice, "no one, including ghosts, can be in this classroom without permission from the principal."

The burst of laughter from the class put the problem to rest.

Thursday continued without further incident until just before the final bell rang. Fern Stewart, the principal, came trudging up the stairs and into the classroom. She looked back over her shoulder as though she were expecting something or somebody.

In a moment a man came thumping up the stairs, a hammer dangled from a loop on the side of his overalls.

"This is Mr. Morgan. As soon as you leave today, he will put up a new chalkboard here on your side wall. As you can see the old one is in bad shape. Please take down your posters and other materials carefully and you can put it all back up tomorrow."

"Oh, thank you, Mrs. Stewart," said Miss Wilson.

"Any questions?" asked the principal.

"No, we'll be ready," replied Miss Wilson.

"Mr. Morgan, you can begin to bring your tools and things up into the hall. When the bell rings, there will be a short stampede, but you look big enough to take care of yourself," continued Mrs. Stewart, as she started out the door and down the stairs with Mr. Morgan following.

"All right, class, let's get the old chalkboard ready," said Miss Wilson. "We have less than ten minutes until the bell."

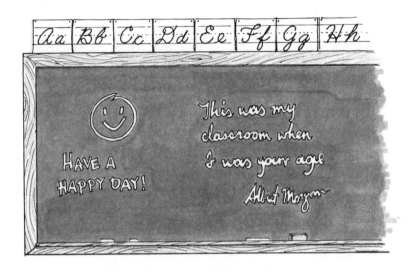

CHAPTER 13

A New Chalkboard and An Old Story

FRIDAY

Friday morning, curiosity had its effect. As Miss Wilson started upstairs, nearly half the class followed her. The new chalkboard was up and everything in the room was neatly in its place. It was downright disappointing until Miss Wilson got to her desk and turned to look at the new chalkboard.

"Ah-h-h, look at that, class," she said almost reverently.

There on the boldly clean and shining new chalkboard was a big smiley face and the words, "HAVE A HAPPY DAY." Farther down, Mr. Morgan had written, "This was my classroom when I was your age," and he had signed it - "Albert Morgan."

The children were impressed. "Miss Wilson, let's leave it there for a while," said Trisha Warren. "We like it."

"All right. I like the note too. We can leave it all day at least."

"Yeah," replied the class.

"Trish, will you write Mr. Morgan a 'Thank You' note for the chalkboard and the greeting?" suggested Miss Wilson.

"Let's all sign it," said Kevin.

The class all agreed. By noon, it was done and the letter given to the principal for delivery to Mr. Morgan that afternoon when he returned to do another repair downstairs. The fourth grade class felt they had been loved and had responded in kind.

Right after the final bell, Miss Wilson went downstairs to the faculty lounge to make copies of papers she needed for class Monday. After a visit with two other teachers, she went to speak to Mr. Morgan.

"Miss Wilson, I'll treasure this letter from your class. As you know, I have done work like this at the school for many years. I enjoy the boys and girls, and I have a collection of such letters and notes. Some day I plan to put them all into a big scrapbook and present it to the school for the trophy case. Perhaps they can be shown at class reunions many years from now."

"Let me quickly tell you a story about the school and the old hotel that was here before," said Miss Wilson. She finished Mr. Ben's story and the classroom happenings since.

"No, there have been no ghosts here, Miss Wilson. I recall some funny incidents like Mrs. Hawkin's milk goat wandering into the downstairs hall one morning

75

when I was in the third grade."

Miss Wilson laughed.

"Then there was Billy Ross who had two dogs and lived about half a mile from here. One dog was a friendly mongrel pup and the other was a big droopy-faced coonhound with a good nose. The dogs got out one afternoon and that hound tracked Billy to school and right upstairs into your room. I remember we were into an arithmetic test when both dogs came bounding into the room."

"How did they get in?" asked Miss Wilson.

"We had no air-conditioning back then. We just left the windows and doors open."

"Oh, yes."

"Well, the playful pup was all over the room, greeting the kids. The class was in an uproar of laughter. Our teacher, Mrs. Calhoun, was raising a fuss trying to get the pup out and the old hound was just enjoying it all, as he sat, cutting loose some big woofs and short howls."

Miss Wilson was laughing to tears. "What happened?"

"We all had to go downstairs and out in the yard to get the dogs out. Mrs. Calhoun sent Billy home with the dogs. That was the only way she could get rid of them. She was angry at first, but finally she got tickled and we all had a big laugh."

"I'm keeping you from your work, Mr. Morgan. Thank you for being yourself and for a good story to tell my class, too." She returned to her classroom still laughing.

As she approached the top of the stairs, she heard a little rustling noise in her classroom, then silence.

"What was that?" she thought aloud. Stepping into

the room, she saw small items scattered around under students' desks again. Her smile was now a frown. She tidied up, put her papers on top of the storage cabinet, got her purse and left. Once again, she told herself to stop thinking what she was thinking.

CHAPTER 14

The Ghost Returns

MONDAY MORNING

Miss Wilson found many of her papers from atop the storage cabinet scattered on the floor. Again the floor was cluttered with things from inside the students' desks. She was still standing at her desk, stunned, when the first students began to come into the room.

"What happened, Miss Wilson?" asked Linda Ogden, with an amazed tone in her voice.

"I don't know. We may have a prankster," she replied, shaking her head.

"Wow!" said David, as he entered the room.

Chester, who was right behind David, started backing out of the room.

Kelly was already at his desk when he spied Chester. "Look, look, Chester is scared."

"No, I'm not!" responded Chester angrily.

"Admit it, Chester, you're scared!" taunted Kelly. "Chicken!"

"That's enough, Kelly." Miss Wilson's stern voice settled the matter. "Get to your desk, Chester. Everyone settle down and let's pick things up."

"Yes, ma'am," said Chester, as he moved cautiously to his desk.

The cleanup activity was halted again when Kim held up a tiny brown object and asked, "What is this?" Everyone stared.

"Looks like a nut, but I've never seen one like it," said Miss Wilson.

"About like a jumping bean," said Viki Cantu. "My Uncle Francisco brings them from Mexico sometimes. No, I don't think that's what it is."

"Here is another one," said Andy Schultz.

Miss Wilson took them both. "I'll look into it," she said. "They are not acorns or chestnuts. We'll find out. Now take your places. Everyone here? No, Reuben Lewis isn't here. Oh, yes, he and his mother have gone to be with his father whose Navy ship is in port for just a week."

"Miss Wilson," said Annie Johnson, with a little quiver in her voice. "Do we have a ghost in here?"

"No, I don't think so."

"I'm scared," said Annie.

"I think somebody is playing tricks on us. What do you think?" asked Miss Wilson, looking confidently around the room.

David held up his hand.

"Yes, David."

"I took the old photograph back to Mr. Ben Saturday and I told him what happened last week. Mr. Ben only laughed and said, 'I don't believe in ghosts, David, but I'll tell you this. The old chief didn't talk much, but he was gracious and well-liked. If he is your ghost, I assure you he is a friendly one.'"

"Oh, well," said Miss Wilson, with a smile. "If we do have a ghost, let's enjoy him. After all, we may be the only fourth grade in the whole world with our own friendly ghost."

This brought some laughter. Chester didn't laugh.

"Relax, Chester," taunted Kelly, "it is just some dirty dog playing tricks on us."

"Hush, Kelly. Oh, yes. Dogs! I have a funny story to tell you. Mr. Morgan told me about it, Friday." Miss Wilson was eager to change the subject. The class delighted in the stories about the goat and the dogs.

At noon, Kevin Carlson stayed to speak to Miss Wilson. "I help my dad set camera traps to get pictures of wild birds and animals. May I bring a camera and set a trap in here to see who is making the mess?"

Miss Wilson looked at Kevin thoughtfully a long moment. "Kevin, this is getting worse every day. I've got to stop it; it's too much distraction. I think not. It would be even more distracting. But, thank you, and I will keep it in mind."

"Yes, ma'am," said Kevin, disappointed. He went on to lunch, but could not forget his idea.

The class remained in a strange mood all day. The tiny jumping beans, or whatever they were, made an excellent mystery and the idea of a friendly ghost was a super subject for active minds. As the day ended, Miss Wilson decided they should discuss the subject again.

"Class, let's not jump to conclusions and get ourselves laughed at." She paused. "I still think someone may be doing this to us as a joke. Let's keep it to ourselves and see if we can get to the bottom of this. Okay?"

Most of the class nodded.

"Let's not get caught in a trap. Anyway, ghosts never hurt anyone. Right?"

"Right," said David. "Mr. Ben said so too."

The bell rang.

"Until tomorrow, girls and boys. Have a nice evening. Kevin, see me a minute before you leave, please."

With everyone gone, Kevin came to Miss Wilson's desk. "Yes, ma'am?"

"You may have a solution, Kevin. Are you sure you can do this?"

"Yes, ma'am, we do it a lot. I have some good pictures I have done myself."

"Bring them to show us some day, Kevin."

"Oh, sure, I'd like that."

"How would you do it here, Kevin?"

"I would put the camera up on the cabinet between some books and aim it to look out across the room. Then I would run the trip wire along the desks over by the windows and across between the desks. Whoever comes in will strike the wire out there and trip the camera."

"Let's try it, Kevin. But bring all your things in a paper bag tomorrow and tell no one. If we have a prankster, he or she must not know about it. Understand?"

"Yes, ma'am. Wow!! This will be fun!"

CHAPTER 15

A Secret Plan

TUESDAY MORNING

Most of the class went upstairs with Miss Wilson. The puzzling fourth grade mystery had all of them excited with the great adventure. Little things were scattered about again, and one more little brown nut or bean was on the floor by the cabinet. As usual, nothing was broken nor missing.

Miss Wilson greeted the class and closed the door. "Class, listen to me, this is important. I think someone who knows about Karen and David's report is trying to frighten us. Now, let's turn the tables on whoever it is. Can all of you keep a secret?"

The class agreed with solemn nods.

"We have a plan, but it won't work if anyone other than this class knows about it. You must not tell anyone or even talk about it between yourselves outside of this room. Now, if you will promise to keep our secret, hold up your hand."

Hands went up all over the room.

"Hold them up, please. Chester, have you made up your mind? All right then, everyone promises. Keep them up. Look around the room. You are promising one another too. Thank you."

She picked up Kevin's paper bag. "This is Kevin's camera that he and his father use to set camera traps for pictures of wild animals and birds. Right after school today, Kevin will set it up here so we will get a picture of our prankster."

"Oh boy!" exclaimed David.

The class chattered in their excitement.

"Now, let's go on with our business today in a normal way. Don't let anyone suspect that we have a plan, okay? Let's see some hands on that. Fine, let's go to work."

As soon as the building was quiet after the last bell, Miss Wilson closed the door and Kevin went to work. The camera was placed on the storage cabinet and supported by two stacks of books. Kevin ran his tiny trip wire across the cabinet, down to the latch, over to the corner desk, down the row by the windows to the center desk, then across all the aisles in the room. He tied it off to the center desk by the chalkboard.

Kevin set the camera without film. He tested the wire in each of the aisles. Just a little pressure snapped the camera and flash. Each time the camera recocked itself ready for another picture.

"It works fine, Miss Wilson." Kevin inserted a twelve exposure roll of film, set the focus for the middle of the room and propped the camera carefully in place. They went out of the room quietly.

CHAPTER 16

Tripped Trap and A Jig

WEDNESDAY MORNING

The whole class waited outside the school building for Miss Wilson to arrive. Never had anyone seen this group so quiet. Kevin and Miss Wilson led the parade up the stairs. They all paused at the door to survey the room. Once again the floor was cluttered with items from inside the desks, but again there was nothing broken or missing.

Kevin checked his camera. "Wow! Every picture is snapped, the whole roll. I can't believe this!" he exclaimed.

"How many pictures is that, Kevin?"

"Twelve, Miss Wilson."

"This doesn't make sense. Who would stay around

and trip a flash camera twelve times?"

"I don't know."

"Maybe our prankster figured it out and did this to fool us," suggested Scott.

"This is strange, girls and boys." Miss Wilson looked puzzled. "But, let's play it out. Kevin, give me the film. I'll get it developed at the new film shop after school. Now back to business. Let's tidy up and go on as usual. Keep your cool, say nothing to anyone, and we will look at our pictures all together here first thing in the morning."

"I can't wait," said a squirming Kim.

"Kevin, you did fine, - - - I think," said Miss Wilson with a little laugh. "Now, listen to me carefully. Right now we have either a prankster or a friendly ghost. Either way, there is no reason for alarm."

"This is a great mystery, Miss Wilson. It's fun!" said Eddie Vickers.

"Well, yes, it is fun, come to think of it. Weird, but fun," she said, then looked over the class thoughtfully. "Do you think it's fun? Hold up your hands if you think so."

All hands went up, some slowly, and Chester was last.

"Let's keep it fun and secret just a little longer. Here we go, back to work until tomorrow."

It took lots of winks and understanding smiles all day to keep wonder and anticipation from being overcome by imagination.

When the final bell rang, there was not the usual rush out of the room. Everyone stayed and spoke quietly to one another as they gathered around Miss Wilson. Finally she smiled and made a silly face and said, "Fun, isn't it? I can't wait either."

She grabbed her purse and the film, smiled again and rushed for the door. "I'm on my way," she shouted and danced a comical little jig as she stepped outside the door.

By the stairs stood the janitor, who had just come up with his arms full of brooms, mops and a bucket. "This is my day to mop your room," he said, then looked at her, smiling. "Do you always go home this excited, Miss Wilson?"

Miss Wilson stopped to laugh at the whole outrageous scene. "No, Mr. Pitts, today is special," she replied, and paused to think what else to say. She felt foolish, but didn't want to explain. Suddenly she danced another little jig and said, "But, let's enjoy this one while it lasts," and hurried on down the stairs.

A parade of giggling, laughing children followed her out of the school.

David sat on the bench, still smiling about Miss Wilson's little jigs. Karen called to him from the corner as she pointed up. "There is Mr. Ben's friend, the squirrel again, David."

"Yeah, sure is." He watched the squirrel scamper along the cable. When the squirrel was right overhead, David said, "Hi, Squirrel!" The squirrel stopped and was still looking down at David when his mother drove up.

CHAPTER 17

Growing Mystery and
A Whistling Exit

THURSDAY MORNING

Miss Wilson's waiting class gathered to follow her up the stairs. This most unusual morning ritual drew attention from other teachers and students who stood in the downstairs hall, watching the show. Miss Wilson stopped halfway up to smile and wave at the group. Her class turned and waved, too. No one smiled or waved back. Muffled little snickers revealed the fourth graders were enjoying the secret, the suspense, and their growing mystique.

To everyone's surprise, the room was neat and orderly. Not one thing was out of place. The freshly scrubbed floors made the room seem uncomfortably tidy. Once again there was a feeling of disappointment as though they had been betrayed.

"Well," said Miss Wilson, as she looked around, "I didn't expect this. But I do have some news. Mr. Watkins at the garden and feed store says these little brown nuts are chinquapins."

"What are chinquapins?" asked Sandy.

"They are a type of dwarf chestnut that grows wild on bushes in some parts of the country. I have to tell you Mr. Watkins said they are popular with kids and were a regular food for Indians. They have never been sold in the markets."

The silent students began to look at one another with raised eyebrows.

In a moment, Kevin broke the tension. "Let us see the pictures please, Miss Wilson."

Miss Wilson closed the door. "Gather around and I will show you," said Miss Wilson. "These are confusing at best. We got nothing recognizable."

"Oh!" said Karen, with a disappointed frown.

Miss Wilson started laying the pictures on her desk. "This one shows nothing but an empty room. A good picture though, Kevin. Here is another with nothing unusual and a third one with nothing. This one shows a fuzzy white blur over the whole right side. Here are two more with similar blurs."

"I don't understand these," said Kevin very thoughtfully. "This never happened before."

"All the rest have a similar shapeless blur in the corner, on the bottom, different places. This last one is almost solid white," she explained. "We got something, but I don't know what it is."

"It's the ghost," said Chester in a shakey subdued voice. "I know it is."

With the air heavy with suspense and mystery, the

class studied the pictures. One by one the snapshots were passed around for closer looks.

"Have any of you ever seen a picture of a ghost, in a book or anywhere?"

No one responded.

"I don't know of any ghost pictures that are not seriously disputed," said Miss Wilson. "I still believe we have someone very real playing a trick on us. Some folks argue there are no ghosts, so you can't get a picture of one. They believe what is seen is imagined and exists only in the viewer's mind."

She looked over the questioning faces of the class. "Now, here are our pictures; some of nothing and others of something that we can't recognize. I don't know what this is telling us, but we will find out."

"Ghosts are white," said Chester with a shaky voice. "Those are white ghosts in the picture."

"I don't agree, Chester, but I am sure that whoever it is, it or he or she means us no harm. So, let's enjoy the mystery of it and continue to wonder and search until we know the answer."

Kevin raised his hand. "Miss Wilson, may I have my father look at the pictures?"

"Of course, Kevin, and tell him the truth about them. Also ask him to keep all this to himself until we know what is happening."

"Yes, ma'am."

Mr. Pitts, the janitor, was at the fourth grade door again at the final bell. "Came to see your little jig again, Miss Wilson," he said.

"This isn't a jig day, Mr. Pitts," explained Miss Wilson with a chuckle. "But if you will keep smiling, we'll whistle our way out today." She began to whistle a little tune softly.

"My day to clean your windows," explained the janitor. "Guess I'll whistle while I work too." He began to whistle along with a few students who could stop laughing long enough to pucker and tweet.

For the moment, the ghost was forgotten and the day came to a happy end.

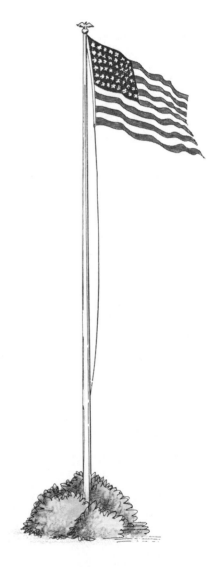

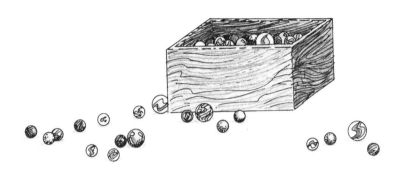

CHAPTER 18

Whistling In and Screaming Out

FRIDAY MORNING

Silent parades of teacher-led students are common during the day, but such scenes before the first bell are a rare curiosity. The rest of the school was waiting to watch this rare event again Friday morning. Miss Wilson saw the awed crowd waiting in the downstairs hall. Instead of going directly into the building, she detoured across to the flagpole and motioned to her class to follow. The alert students quickly gathered around her.

"Good morning, class," she said. "Our morning behavior this past week has our schoolmates wondering why we are so mysterious. Everyone is waiting and watching this morning. Let's make the most of it, shall we?"

Snickers and giggles signaled approval.

"We left whistling yesterday, let's return the same way. You all know how the elves whistled on their way to work. A little swagger makes it all work better, so follow my lead. All together now."

She danced a little step from side to side and stepped off whistling and swaggering her way to work. The class picked up the tune and the walk, and fell into line. The day was off to a good start.

Upstairs, the room was again neat and undisturbed. Most everyone except Chester seemed disappointed. Their ghost wasn't being friendly any more. The class was quiet in wonder.

"Well, girls and boys, perhaps our prankster or would-be ghost has tired of the charade. This is two days with no problems. But let's not give up our vigilance. Kevin, what did your father say about the pictures?"

"He is out of town, Miss Wilson, and he won't be back until Wednesday. His work is like that."

"Oh, that is a disappointment," exclaimed Miss Wilson. "I have an uncle who is a photographer. I will mail him a set of prints tomorrow. Perhaps he can explain our ghost pictures. Now, it's back to work."

All day Friday everything was normal. Miss Wilson reminded the class that they should set their clocks back one hour Sunday morning for the time change from daylight saving time to standard time. She explained that the one-hour change for the days with less daylight were for those who must start work early. "This way they will not begin in the dark. School children who live far away from the school should not walk nor wait for a bus in the dark either, so the time change is necessary for everyone's safety."

Chester gave the first history report during the last period. He had a large box containing a collection of marbles that his grandfather started as a boy in school. Chester explained that marbles were first made of marble in ancient times, then of fired clay and crystal glass. Chester passed around samples of those and the newer ones as they appeared through the years. He showed the early crockies, agates, solids, clears, steelies (which are really ball bearings), and the marblized glass ones in many sizes and colors that are common yet today.

"Many years ago school grounds had bare sandy areas just for children to play marbles and tops," explained Chester. "But today, I will only tell you about marbles."

"Marble games varied from school to school. Also some of the names for things were different. The marble you shot with was always your favorite one and it was called your taw. Everybody picked something really different for their taw, so they were never mixed up about whose taw was where," explained Chester.

Chester drew a big circle on the blackboard and explained the basic game of marbles. Then he drew the overlapping half circles and variations, and the hole pattern for the game of holes or "holies" as it was sometimes called. He went on to explain the lag line and demonstrated several popular ways to shoot.

"Playing marbles is a lost art because we have so many new toys today," explained Chester. "Back in the old days, Grandpa says there was a season for each game every year. Marbles were mostly played in elementary schools. The year started with marble season, then on to tops as the weather got cold and the ground got wet. There were winter games too in each school. In the spring, it was back to tops as the season warmed up and again to marbles on the dry ground before school was out for summer vacation."

The class enjoyed the magnificent assortment of old marbles and passed them around for a closer look. They raised many questions about the games and shared comments about Chester's report.

"That was an excellent report, Chester," said Miss Wilson. "You are right, not many children today even know how to shoot a marble. Thank you. Now, Linda, it is your turn."

Chester placed his box of marbles on the floor by the storage cabinet and returned to his seat.

Linda had a large 1902 mail order catalog. The photocopies she had made of several selected pages brought on lively discussions and a riot of laughter. The questions were both serious and funny. When the final bell rang, the children were still enjoying the old catalog.

"Excellent, Linda, this was very good. Don't forget to set your clocks back Sunday. Have a good week-end," said Miss Wilson.

The class drifted out of the room and down the stairs, still laughing and joking about the grand old mail order catalog.

As Miss Wilson followed the class down the stairs and out of the building, she stopped a moment to look around. "Chester, you forgot your marbles."

"Oh, yes, Ma'am, thanks." He rushed back up-stairs. As he entered the quiet empty classroom, he began to get a creepy feeling. He eased over to the storage cabinet and stooped over to pick up the box of marbles. Just as he raised up, he heard a little rustle by his ear. He turned to look but a swish of hair brushed across his face.

"Wah-h-h-h - - - Eie-eee-e!" screamed Chester with all his might. By the time he took a breath to let go a second scream, his feet were halfway to the stairs. He grabbed the top handrail post and swung around it to make the turn down the stairs, but his box of marbles didn't make the turn with him.

Chester was nearly to the middle landing of the stairs when the box of marbles exploded against the wall. Chester lost his grip on the post at the landing and ricocheted off the wall. By the time he squalled again and changed directions down the last flight of stairs, a flood of antique marbles was cascading down the stairs behind him. They, too, bounced off the landing wall and continued down the stairs in pursuit of Chester.

"Awieee-eee-e-e-e-e." screamed Chester again as he got to the bottom of the stairs. He tried to turn toward the front door, but lost his balance and tumbled into a squirming heap.

The crowd at the front door listened in horror to Chester's pitiful screams. Miss Wilson and a few brave students rushed in to see what was the matter. They saw poor Chester get to his feet just as the flood of marbles caught up with him. Miss Wilson stopped at a safe distance, but David, Kevin, Shanna, Jennifer and Sandy tried to help Chester. The wreck only got worse. Everyone fell over marbles and one another until they finally worked their way to safe ground out the front door.

Miss Wilson held the shaking Chester in her arms to help him collect himself. Her assurances and understanding hugs finally put Chester together again. It took a while longer for him to talk.

"The ghost!" blurted Chester, and choked up again. He shivered and quaked violently.

"Take your time, Chester, take your time."

"I - - -, I- - -, I heard something and then, and then, yi-i-i-i - - - - and then his hair swished across my face. And, and - - - aww-w-w-w, ughh-h-h-h - I ran and I ran - eee - - - wah -h-h."

"Yes, Chester, of course - anyone would run," assured Miss Wilson.

"I just picked up my marbles and I heard this noise

as I stood up and then, swish." He motioned across his face with his hand. Chester continued to shake with fear.

"Yes, I see," said Miss Wilson.

By now a small crowd had gathered and the fourth grade ghost story was being repeated excitedly. Mr. Pitts stood in the school door, leaning on a broom, watching the happenings. "Miss Wilson, you had better see Chester home. I'll take care of the marbles."

"Thank you, Mr. Pitts," said Miss Wilson.

"Don't you worry, Chester, I'll see that every single one is returned to you. Any of you kids want to help me round them up?" asked Mr. Pitts.

There were no volunteers. The children were all too scared to go back into the schoolhouse.

"Hey, Mr. Ghost," shouted Mr. Pitts, "I have been here a long time. How come you ain't spooked me? Oh! You don't like me, that it?" He continued to ramble on loudly at and about the ghost as he began herding the scattered marbles together with his push-broom.

Miss Wilson walked Chester home and explained to his mother.

CHAPTER 19

The Ghost Story Explodes

FRIDAY, After School

Excitement was growing as the story spread rapidly across town. When Winnie Wilson got home, from Chester's house, Mrs. Stewart, the principal, and the superintendent, Mr. Kilgore, were waiting on her front porch. Her telephone was ringing as she invited them inside.

"Let the telephone ring for now, Miss Wilson," said Mr. Kilgore. "Folks want some facts and answers, so let's get organized and be prepared to tell them what they need to know."

"Let's go back to my class room right now," suggested Miss Wilson.

"That is a good idea," said the principal.

The telephone stopped ringing. Mr. Kilgore picked it up quickly and started dialing. "I'm going to ask Sheriff Johnson to meet us there."

When Miss Wilson, Mrs. Stewart and Mr. Kilgore reached the school, the sheriff was already waiting upstairs for them.

Mr. Pitts walked in with Chester's box of marbles. "Chester sure had lots of marbles, Miss Wilson, and I can't believe how far they scattered," he said.

"Those are his grandfather's collection that he started as a little boy," she told him.

"You know I've enjoyed this. There are marbles here like I have never seen before and then many like those we bought at Mr. Ben's store when I was a boy. The box isn't hurt. I put them back into it."

"Thank you for taking care of them, Mr. Pitts. Just put the box on my desk, please."

"Mr. Pitts, have you seen or heard anything unusual in here this evening?" asked the superintendent.

"No, not a thing today, or any other day, for that matter. I don't understand the ghost problem either."

"Let's review it all please, Miss Wilson," continued Mr. Kilgore.

Miss Wilson went over the whole story, and ended by saying, "Now, I haven't believed in ghosts and still don't. I think I had most of my students agreeing with me until this incident. I'm afraid I am back at square one again."

"Miss Wilson, I can see now you should have asked for help sooner, but I think I would have done about the same things you did. I understand your principal has already said she believes as you do that we are dealing with a very clever prankster," said the superintendent.

"Perhaps we can help with that," interrupted the sheriff. "I will be here early Monday to check the building before classes begin, and I will keep a deputy here all day, watching everything in the halls during and after school."

"Thank you, Sheriff Johnson. This will put most parents at ease," said Mr. Kilgore. "Let's call a meeting in the auditorium of all the teachers in this school and all concerned parents at seven o'clock, Monday evening."

"I'll be there, too," said the sheriff. "By then, we may know more. We'll go to work on it, too."

"Excellent, Sheriff. Now I propose we maintain our position that there is no ghost, but we do have a disturbing problem and we will solve it," continued the superintendent.

"I think this is reasonable," said Mrs. Stewart. "Our telephones will be busy this weekend. Shall we invite everyone interested to the meeting then?"

"Yes, perhaps we should. I will see that the story and meeting announcement get into the Sunday paper," said the superintendent.

After looking over Miss Wilson's room carefully and finding nothing unusual, they went home.

All the talk created an exciting weekend for the kids.

CHAPTER 20

The Ghost Appears

MONDAY MORNING

Early Monday morning, Sheriff Johnson, three deputies, the superintendent, the principal, all the teachers and six worried parents inspected every room, closet, nook and cranny in the schoolhouse before the first student arrived.

Only the fourth grade classroom had small things from the students' desks scattered around again. This was promptly set in order.

The inspection group members stayed to reassure parents and students alike until the school was settled into the regular routine. The students enjoyed all the whispering and wandering adults patrolling the halls and peeking into the classrooms. By noon only Deputy Kern continued to roam the halls.

Reuben was back and enjoying all the unusual excitement.

As the day neared its end, the whole school was almost back to normal with students relaxed into the afternoon slump.

Ten minutes into Beth Fallon's history report, Karen's eye caught a movement outside. She looked out the window to see Mr. Ben's friendly squirrel scampering along the telephone and television cables going to the school. She smiled as the squirrel jumped off into the big oak tree and scooted down the limbs out of her sight. About two minutes later Karen's eye picked up movement again as he darted up the tree and leaped back onto the wires. The squirrel paused to rest and seemed to be looking right at Karen. Well, thought Karen, you are early today and what are you doing over here?

The squirrel flipped his tail nervously as he peered at the windows. He started slowly toward the school building again.

Suddenly Karen remembered. No, she thought, you aren't early, we are late because of the time change. So this is where you were going every afternoon.

Karen's desk by the window let her watch the squirrel as he made his way along the wire. Before he disappeared above the window, he stopped to look down again. He flipped his bushy tail just as the sun came from behind a cloud. The sunlight passing through his tail produced a flash of brilliant fluffy copper color, then he was out of sight up under the roof somewhere.

Karen smiled at the quiet little circus she had witnessed. The fluffy flash of sunlight on the squirrel's tail stuck in her mind. Why do I keep seeing that? she thought. Yes, it reminds me of something. She concentrated on that until in her memory she suddenly saw the blurred picture of the old grave stone. She was about to tell herself this was silly when she remembered Kevin's ghost pictures, the white fluffy ones especially. Her mind was quickly racing through the happenings in the classroom. Of course, she thought, and turned to stare at the storage cabinet, remembering Kevin's camera trap.

As she looked, Karen heard a little rustling noise and the squirrel peeked out at her from behind George Washington's picture.

"I see the ghost, right there!" blurted Karen, pointing excitedly at the cabinet. Her words were explosive.

The squirrel was surprised by the unexpected presence of the class and Karen's outburst. He scampered back the way he came.

Chester screamed and dashed out of the room, only to collide with Deputy Kern as he hurried into the classroom. Chester recovered himself and raced on down the stairs and out of the school, still yelling.

The deputy rushed in to see what was happening. The wide-eyed students seemed frozen in their seats. A few had taken refuge under their desks.

"What is it? Where is it?" barked Deputy Kern.

Karen was too excited to say sensible words. "There! right there — he was on the cabinet!"

CHAPTER 21

Karen Spots the Ghost

MONDAY

Everyone stared at the cabinet in stunned silence, then Miss Wilson, David, Kim, Jennifer, Shanna and several others rushed to Karen's side.

"I don't see anything," said Miss Wilson.

Deputy Kern was looking frantically around the room.

"I guess I scared him away," declared Karen.

The principal and two more teachers raced into the room, too short of breath to speak after rushing up the stairs.

"Karen," said Miss Wilson, sternly, "are you - - -?"

"There he goes!" shouted Karen, pointing out the window. "See, we frightened him away!"

They all turned to look out the windows.

"Where? Where?" demanded Deputy Kern.

"The squirrel - - on the wires!" replied Karen.

For an instant no one said a word. Then everyone turned to Karen who bravely sat upright in her desk. The deputy, the teachers and the principal looked at one another in shocked relief that slowly began to turn into stern disgust.

"Karen," said Miss Wilson again, "what do you mean?"

"It's him, Miss Wilson - - - I know it's him!" Karen was positive.

"A squirrel is <u>not</u> a ghost," scolded Mrs. Stewart in her most authoritative voice.

Deputy Kern was pacing back and forth, shaking his head in disbelief.

The class sat in stunned silence.

"No, no, Mrs. Stewart, he's what we thought was a ghost," explained Karen.

Deputy Kern looked out the window at the fleeing squirrel, then up at the wires again. He rubbed his chin thoughtfully.

Mrs. Stewart was growing more upset. "Young lady, you are trying my patience."

"Wait a minute," interrupted the deputy. "Karen, where did you see the squirrel?"

"First out there on the wires. We see him most every day after school, but out front. I thought he was early today, but then I remembered we are late because of the time change."

"Karen," demanded the principal. "I - - - - -."

"Wait a moment, please, ma'am," pleaded Deputy Kern, as he held his hand up for silence. "Where did you see him when you said that you saw the ghost?"

"He looked at me from behind George Washington's big picture, right there." She pointed at the picture.

Deputy Kern took the picture off the cabinet. There were gasps as everyone saw a rectangular hole cut neatly in the wall behind it.

"What is this?" asked the deputy. "It sure is squirrel size."

"Oh, that is for the new TV cable," said the principal.

Deputy Kern studied the hole in the wall a moment. "Perhaps he got into the attic where the wires come into the building, then came down into the wall where the new TV cable will go, and out this hole."

There was a quiet pause.

"All right, now I'm sure Karen did see the squirrel in here," continued Deputy Kern, "and I think she is trying to tell us more if we will just listen."

"Go ahead, Karen," assured Miss Wilson.

"When he came by up there on the wire, there was a fuzzy flash of sunlight through his tail. That reminded me of the fuzzy white pictures Kevin took in his camera trap. Then I remembered the tombstone picture that was blurred because it was out of focus. When I looked at the cabinet where Kevin's camera had been, I heard a noise and saw the squirrel. Then I knew he was our ghost."

"Oh, sure," exclaimed Kevin, "I focused for out here in the room and when he tripped the wire up on the cabinet we took a picture of his tail."

"Yeah," said Karen, "and it blurred."

"Sure, that explains the fuzzy white pictures."

"What about the others?" asked David.

"I don't know," said Kevin. "Could we see a squirrel on the floor if he tripped the wire? Let's look at the pictures."

Miss Wilson got the photographs from her desk. Kevin and Deputy Kern studied them carefully.

"It would be almost impossible to see him if he were on the floor," said the deputy. "The desks are in the way. Wait, there, in this one, I believe I see the tip of his tail between the desks."

"I think so too," said Kevin.

"Let me see," said Miss Wilson, "yes, you are right. We didn't see it because we didn't know what to look for."

"Why did he keep coming back here?" asked the principal.

"For the pecans," said Karen. "Annie gave us all pecans when she made her report. We put them in our desks."

"Of course," sighed Miss Wilson. "My pecans on top of the cabinet were the first ones he got. We should have guessed."

"That doesn't explain the chinquapins," said Annie.

"Chinquapins!" exclaimed Reuben. "Did he get my chinquapins?" He rushed to his desk and dug frantically in it.

"That rascal got every one." He held up a small mangled and quite empty paper sack.

They all began to laugh at Reuben's dismay. The whole scary mystery was getting funny now.

"Reuben has been away for a week. He didn't know about the chinquapins we found and we didn't know he had them," explained Miss Wilson.

"Uncle Joseph sends me some every year. I forgot I put them here. I like to eat them walking home after school," explained Reuben.

David went over to the storage cabinet and stood, hands on his hips, thinking for a moment. "Chester's box of marbles was here. He picked them up like this." David stooped over and picked up an imaginary box. "Chester heard a noise here as he raised up. He turned in time for the frightened squirrel to turn and flee, and - - - SWISH - goes a tail across Chester's face."

"Oh heavens!" gasped Miss Wilson, "we forgot about Chester. That poor boy must have run all the way home by now."

The school secretary, who had joined the noisy group, spoke up. "Winnie, I know Chester and where he lives. I'll go. You stay here and take care of your class."

"Oh, thank you, Diana," replied Miss Wilson. "You better hurry on. That boy was awfully frightened."

Deputy Kern scratched his chin as he considered all the facts versus the new explanations. "I believe there were days when the ghost or the squirrel did not come into the class room. Can we explain that?" he asked.

"Let's see if we can," said Miss Wilson. "Who remembers the first day there was no mess?"

"I keep a diary," said Ruth Sellers. "I'll check it." She got a little notebook from her desk and began to turn the pages. "Friday before last Friday, there was nothing," she said.

"Anyone imagine why?" asked the deputy.

The boys and girls looked at one another for an answer, but came up with nothing.

"What else is in your diary for that day and perhaps the day before?"

"We had a new chalkboard Friday."

"I know," said Jason. "Mr. Morgan was working in here when we left Thursday. He must have frightened the squirrel away."

"Okay, that makes sense," said Deputy Kern. "Let's check the other times."

"Last Thursday and Friday, there was no mess. Miss Wilson reminded us we had two days without the ghost," said Scott. "Remember?

"That is correct, Scott! Thank you!" said Miss Wilson. "Now, why?"

"You jigged Wednesday and whistled Thursday, Miss Wilson, remember?" said Vicki, with a giggle.

"Yes, yes, of course," said Miss Wilson. She laughed. "Mr. Pitts scrubbed our floors after school Wednesday and cleaned our windows Thursday. So then, the squirrel wouldn't come on in with someone here and we had no mess Thursday nor Friday, but we did again today."

"All right now," said the deputy, very seriously. "Is there anything that we have not explained?"

No one seemed to have any more ideas or questions.

"Is there anyone who is not satisfied the squirrel was our ghost?" asked the principal.

Everyone looked thoughtful and serious, but no one answered.

"Officer, shall we declare the 'Case of The Haunted Classroom' closed?" asked Mrs. Stewart.

"Indeed," replied Deputy Kern. "Who would have ever thought that one old squirrel could fool and upset so many people? I will never forget this one."

"The squirrel didn't do this alone," said Miss Wilson. "Our own imaginations helped a lot."

"I think we owe Karen an apology," said Mrs.

Stewart. "Forgive us, Karen, and thank you for your observations and explanation. That was excellent."

Miss Wilson was nodding in agreement. "I'm proud of you, too, Karen," she said.

After a moment of relieved silence, Miss Wilson said, "So, we didn't really have a ghost after all. But we all came to like Chief Longhair. I will say that, in spirit, he is still with us and he will always be our friend."

"Come here, Winnie," said the principal, very sternly.

Miss Wilson looked puzzled, but walked over to Mrs. Stewart, who put her hand on Miss Wilson's shoulder. "Now I have just one more thing to say to all of you."

"Yes?" said Miss Wilson, as she turned a quizzical look at the principal who was looking back out of the corner of her eyes.

"Well - - - just this - - -, Winnie, you are a very special teacher. I am proud of the way you handled this whole thing. Your understanding and control in this exciting learning experience for your class has been excellent. That squirrel upset us all, but you managed it very well. Your patience and even your humor were delightful. This fourth grade class is very lucky to have you."

The class gave a cheer for Miss Wilson. She gave them a big smile as her relief turned into well-earned pride.

One by one, they all began to laugh. No one heard the final bell ring over the merriment.

As David came out of the school, he spied his mother in the station wagon waiting by the bench. He ran up to the window, "Mom, you won't believe this.

I can't wait to tell you - - -!"

"I have news, too, David. Get in the back," said Nancy.

David yanked the back door open and jumped in, letting his books slide across the seat ahead of him. He grabbed for the seat belts, "Mom, let me tell you - - -!"

There was a lick on his ear. Startled, he turned in time to get a lick on his nose, as the collie puppy with the white front feet bounded across the back seat into his lap.

CHAPTER 22

Introducing the Ghost

THE MONDAY EVENING MEETING

The school auditorium filled rapidly Monday evening. It seemed everyone knew about the squirrel, but this was such a good story, people of all ages and interests wanted to hear more about the whole affair.

"Thank all of you for coming," said Mr. Kilgore. "This meeting was called at a moment of troubled concern. We were puzzled and a little frightened. And now that the mystery is solved and we can laugh about it, we invite all of you to enjoy a review of this exciting little adventure with us."

Muffled chuckles, laughter and a little applause came from the audience. Mr. Kilgore held up his hand for silence. "Most of you already know the highlights of our story. Let me introduce you to those who lived it."

He called Miss Wilson first, explaining she was the heroine of the story for her calm and loving leadership through all the happenings. This brought applause for the proud and relieved teacher.

The introduction of David and Karen as excellent story researchers and perhaps overly effective reporters gained more appreciative chuckles and applause.

"Now, I would like to introduce the squirrel. Mr. Squirrel, will you please stand up and come to the front?"

Everyone looked about the room with expectant smiles, quiet little snickers and snorts.

"That is the spooky trouble with squirrels," said Mr. Kilgore, with a loud sigh. "They are never where you expect them to be and the sneaky little rascals are so blooming hard to see."

Mr. Kilgore waited patiently for the gales of laughter from the crowd to calm down.

"Now, let me introduce an old friend who has recently returned to our town and is the source of the truthful and wonderful story that began our little adventure, Mr. Ben Swain."

As Mr. Ben headed for the stage everyone stood to welcome him. All along the way came handshakes and hugs from eager friends.

Miss Wilson retold the story and called upon each person who was involved to tell his part. Everyone was fascinated with the story of the Indian chief and the old hotel. They marveled at the stories of ghostly happenings and David's observation of the tree, the rock and the fourth grade location. Moans of sympathy for Chester, delighted giggles at the jigs and whistling, and awe at Kevin's clever camera trap revealed the interest of the audience. Karen's observation, memory and quick imagination in solving the mystery brought a standing applause.

Mr. Kilgore closed the meeting by saying, "Thank all of you again for caring and coming here tonight. I am proud of Miss Wilson, the school staff and, of course, the students. You girls and boys were great. Now I bid you 'Good Evening' and send you home to consider one last question. Was this more exciting than any two Halloweens you can remember?"

CHAPTER 23

Ghostly Friends Forever

TUESDAY MORNING

Tuesday, a very subdued and shy Chester was back at school. All morning, Chester didn't say a word; he was too embarrassed to look at or speak to anyone.

As the class came into the room after lunch, David, Reuben, Stephen, Scott, Kelly, Jason and several other boys were waiting for him. Chester looked frightened.

"Chester," said David, "we have two things to say to you. We would like to learn to play marbles and tops if you will teach us. And second, we would like to be your friends."

For a moment Chester was stunned, then he began to smile and shake hands with each of the boys.

Miss Wilson looked on with a smile too.

* * *

Near the end of social studies class that afternoon, Shanna called the class' attention to the squirrel on the wires outside the classroom window.

"Let's name him, 'Chief,'" she suggested.

With giggles and laughter, the class agreed.

"We can put nuts in the big oak tree for him, too," said Scott.

"I believe I have earned that job," said Chester bravely.

"And I'll bring more pecans," said Annie.

"Oh, wonderful," said Miss Wilson. "You are making me proud of this whole affair. This may be the greatest classroom adventure ever."

"We still love Chief Longhair," said Karen, "and now, with Chief, the squirrel, we will remember him even more. Do you think our Chief likes jerky, crackling bread and peppermint too?"

The class began to laugh.

"Well, I know he likes chinquapins," responded Reuben, in mock disgust.

"And I didn't know history reports could be so exciting," said David.

The bell rang.

The students were in a merry mood as they gathered their things to go home. They milled out of the room and down the stairs still chattering happily.

David and Karen were the last ones out of the classroom. At the door they turned to look back at Miss Wilson. Together they touched their hands to their hearts and waved the chief's special wave. She returned the wave and her heart was warmed in a way she had never felt before.

Winnie Wilson sat alone in the quiet classroom. Her mind and her heart were both content at last. She whispered, "I thank you, God, that I am a teacher; please keep me blessed with kids like these."

Just then she thought she felt a little breeze blow her hair - - - and - - - she believed she smelled peppermint. "Yes, Chief, I love them, too," she said, and leaned back in her chair, smiling.

The pleasant aroma of peppermint seemed to grow stronger.

THE KILLJOY CURSE

All Fun Spoilers Be Warned.
Don't tell the secret—Do you hear?
For you will live in fear
IF
You speak my secrets in an unread's ear.
My telltale/tattletail curse
will fall upon you.
Your shadow will shudder,
Your teeth will chatter,
And your tongue will mutter
with dreary, dreary dread.
Your joys will turn to sorrows instead.

My secrets must never be spoken!

Silence!!!

You hear?!!

Mystery Master

Other Children's Books from
NEL-MAR PUBLISHING

SECRETS OF SILVER VALLEY - Ages 7-12
By ZENO ZEPLIN, Illustrated by JUDY JONES
A captivating Hispanic story of mystery, adventure and surprises involving an unusual family. Two orphaned children, Pablo and Elena DeLeon, come to live with an old shepherd, Diego Gonzales. They discover the enchanting hidden secrets of a remote little valley and become a real family in the best sense of the word.

THE HAUNTED CLASSROOM - Ages 9-12
By ZENO ZEPLIN, Illustrated by JUDY JONES
A spooky, funny, wholesome schoolhouse mystery. The fourth grade discovers an ancient haunting where their schoolhouse now stands. Eerie happenings occur which suggest the presence of an Indian chief's ghost in the classroom.

APPLE JACK & THE BIG STORM - Ages 5-10
By JUDY JONES and ZENO ZEPLIN
Approaching wind and rain threaten trouble at Green Apple Farm. Mike and his horse Apple Jack hurry for safety, but Mike gets hurt! Is Apple Jack smart enough and brave enough to get help for his friend?

POPCORN IS MISSING - Ages 7 - 10
By ZENO ZEPLIN, Illustrated by JUDY JONES.
The Town Clowns are Jody and his little dog Popcorn. After a delightful performance at the supermarket, Popcorn disappears. Katy and Beth search for clues and rescue Popcorn.

CLOWNS TO THE RESCUE - Ages 7-10
By ZENO ZEPLIN, Illustrated by BERNICE BROWN
The Town Clowns + 2 performing at the County Fair. Katy and Beth are clowns too. When little Suzan Quinn gets lost, Katy and Beth solve the mystery.

THE CROSS-EYED GHOST - Ages 9 - 14
By ZENO ZEPLIN, Illustrated by JUDY JONES
A whispering, moaning old chimney guards a spooky secret. An eerie light, a black cat, an owl and mystifying events combine in a spooky adventure filled with humor and many surprises.

GREAT TEXAS CHRISTMAS LEGENDS
Ages 9 - 90
By ZENO ZEPLIN, Illustrated by JUDY JONES
Five delightful tales of Christmas Texana for the whole family. Legends of historical places, trains, ships, cowboys, Indians, shrimp boats and more.

SECRET MAGIC - Ages 9 - 13
By ZENO ZEPLIN, Illustrated by JUDY JONES
Lauren must start school far from home, with no friends and no hair. Magic is created with secrets, giving her the love and friendship to cope. An inspiring story for those needing support and those who provide it.

SNOWFLAKE THE GHOST KITTEN -
Ages 7-10
By ZENO ZEPLIN, Illustrated by JUDY JONES
Snowflake was a kitten. Now he is a ghost. The house where he lived is lonely. A family with three little girls is moving in. The fun is about to begin. "Spooking" teaches a real stinker to be a better person. A delightful story of Halloween fun and adventure.

DISCOVERY ON DUSTY CREEK - Ages - 8 - 12
By ZENO ZEPLIN, Illustrated by JUDY JONES
Ginny Brown on a remote ranch searches for arrowheads after a rainstorm. She finds dinosaur bones and begins an exciting adventure.

THE MAGIC CATERPILLAR - Ages 7-10
By and Illustrated by BERNICE BROWN
Friendship is shared by a young boy and a very special caterpillar.

ABOUT THE ILLUSTRATOR

JUDY JONES is a professional artist in Houston, Texas, and a graduate of Texas Academy of Art. After many years of working in the advertising and printing field, she has enjoyed very much illustrating books for Zeno Zeplin. Her own two children and their friends often serve as models. She also welcomes suggestions and responses from the "guest editors" in the schools.

ZENO ZEPLIN

ABOUT THE AUTHOR

Zeno Zeplin, a native Texan, has a B.S. Degree from Texas A & M University and is retired from a professional career in engineering and management. A life-long interest in traveling and history inspired his adventures in writing.

Zeplin started writing stories for his grandchildren. Among Zeplin's children's books are GREAT TEXAS CHRISTMAS LEGENDS, SECRETS OF SILVER VALLEY, and now THE HAUNTED CLASSROOM. His first two books were published at the request of the Texas Sesquicentennial Commission and were official commemoratives.

An inspiration took Zeplin to fourth grade classes for editing some stories. This proved a rewarding experience for both the author and his young "editors". Now Zeno and wife, Margy, (a writing team) go to schools to convince students to believe, "I can write." The Zeplins think the simple "Writing Process," once understood, works for everyone. As writers, they advocate reading and writing as important necessities to live and promote the joys and satisfactions of both. Response from faculty and students to the Zeplins and to Zeno's books has encouraged more stories and books.

NEL-MAR Publishing